"Midnigl

The deep, soft voice was a seductive whisper in Sara's ear. She gasped and straightened abruptly, dropping the container of ice cream she was about to buy back into the freezer.

"Scared, Sara?" he taunted softly, letting his finger trail gently down her jaw and her throat. He stopped to feel the mad thudding of her pulse.

She squeezed her eyes shut. Scared? Terrified was more like it. Terrified that she was too weak to resist the temptation of Dakota Wilder, with his sexy smile and wicked charm. "I have to go now. Excuse me."

"Running again?" he asked huskily.

His touch had burned a fiery path and Sara wondered vaguely how such simple contact could generate so much heat, so much need. The feelings his kiss had aroused in her the previous night came tumbling back. Her breath started to come in shallow gasps, a strange warmth gathered in the pit of her stomach and her knees actually felt weak. She wanted so much....

"This time you won't get away so easily, sweet Sara."

"What if…" Like magic, every time a writer utters these two words—poof!—out comes another story. Salimah Kassam and Lenore Providence, the duo who make up **Selina Sinclair**, have been asking each other "What if…" ever since they started writing their first romance together in seventh-grade English class. Many years and a few attempts later, they sold their Golden Heart finalist manuscript, *A Diamond in the Rough,* to Harlequin Temptation.

Both natives of Toronto, Canada, Salimah and Lenore give a whole new meaning to the term long-distance collaboration. Currently, Salimah is teaching English in northern Pakistan, while Lenore is holding down the fort in Toronto, where she lives with her husband, Miguel, and their toddler, Julianne.

Salimah and Lenore would love to hear from readers. You can write to them c/o Harlequin Books, 225 Duncan Mill Road, Don Mills, Ontario, Canada M3B 3K9.

A DIAMOND
IN THE ROUGH
Selina Sinclair

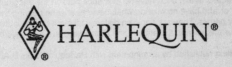

TORONTO • NEW YORK • LONDON
AMSTERDAM • PARIS • SYDNEY • HAMBURG
STOCKHOLM • ATHENS • TOKYO • MILAN • MADRID
PRAGUE • WARSAW • BUDAPEST • AUCKLAND

To our family and friends: Thanks for putting up with the craziness for all these years. To the savvy women and men on Genie's Romance Exchange: Thanks for sharing. To Malle, Birgit and Susan: You guys have *such* good taste!

ISBN 0-373-25788-0

A DIAMOND IN THE ROUGH

Copyright © 1998 by Salimah Kassam & Lenore Timm-Providence.

1

THE SHOT OF WHISKEY left a burning trail down his throat as he tossed it back. There were some things, thought Dakota Wilder, surveying his empty glass with immense satisfaction, worth getting back to civilization for.

Slowly, he lowered the glass onto the table and scanned his surroundings with cold detachment. The bar was dimly lit and smoky, music blared from the jukebox and the Friday-night crowd jumped around on a tiny dance floor in frenzied, X-rated gyrations.

It was a bar like every other he'd seen, except the booze was a little better, the glasses a little cleaner, the people a little richer and the price of pleasure a little higher. Nonetheless, the reason for its popularity was the same.

It was a pickup joint.

His gaze left the dance floor and went on to search the tables scattered around it before shifting back and stopping abruptly. The redhead was moving rhythmically against her partner, but her hungry gaze was trained on Dakota.

He returned her blatant perusal, letting his gaze trail lazily down her tall, slim body and linger appreciatively over her small breasts and long legs. She smiled, tipped her head back and closed her eyes, then licked her lips in slow provocation.

Civilization definitely had its perks.

It had been six long months since he'd had a woman, but if he played his cards right, if his body didn't quit on him, he'd have one tonight.

He smiled with grim determination. Getting up from the bar, he searched through his wallet for a couple of bills, tossed them on top of the counter and headed for the dance floor. He was halfway there when a man's slurred voice made him tense.

"Come on, sugar, just one little dance?"

"No, please, Roy, I'd rather not." A lull in the juke-box allowed Dakota to make out the soft words from the table behind him.

He forced himself to relax. *Keep walking, Wilder.* Whoever she was, she could probably take care of herself without his running interference. Hell, maybe she'd come on to Roy just like the redhead had come on to Dakota and now she was playing hard to get. He'd met too many women like that and saw no reason why this one should be any different.

It was none of his business. He was going to keep walking until he hit the dance floor and then he was going to forget about everything except the warm, willing woman he hoped to have in his arms.

"On your feet, babe. I seen you smiling and batting your pretty little lashes at me from across the room. You sent me an invite, now I wanna party."

"You're hurting me. Please let go of my arm." The words were voiced firmly enough, but Dakota heard the tinge of panic that had crept into them. He tried to ignore the woman's predicament, but the slight quaver in her voice made him hesitate.

He got as far as the next table before stopping and

letting out a heartfelt curse. Then he sighed in resignation and turned back.

He had a feeling he was going to regret this.

SARA MATTHEWS closed her eyes, took a deep breath and tried not to let the threat of impending hysteria overwhelm her. It was hard because, at that moment, a very large drunk named Roy was digging his very large fingers very painfully into her arm.

Suffice it to say that if she had half this Neanderthal's pea-size brain, she wouldn't have come here tonight. But in an alarming attack of temporary insanity, spawned by desperation, she'd convinced herself that all she had to do was put on an act, pretend she was Marilyn Monroe or Madonna or something, and everything would be all right.

But it wasn't all right. It hadn't been anything approaching all right since the moment she'd first walked into the noisy, crowded bar.

She was a lunatic to have come up with such a dumb idea—she'd be the first to admit as much—but then again, she was a desperate woman! After all, there weren't that many places in the town of Beaver Creek, population 1320, to meet the kind of people she needed to meet.

Men people. Big, strong, frightening men people.

And since the ones Kate had told her about in town were either too young, too old or too married for her purposes, she'd been forced to take drastic measures.

Of course, if she'd allowed herself to think about this impulsive plan for more than a minute after her mother's fateful phone call this afternoon, she would never have come here.

But insanity, temporary or otherwise, was hell on the brains.

The proof was in the tightening of Roy's fingers on her arm as he tried to force her up. Eyes still tightly closed, Sara tried desperately to think of how she was going to get out of her latest predicament.

For once, her imagination failed her.

Luckily, fate didn't.

"Looks to me like the lady's not interested." The words were spoken in a pleasant enough manner, but the soft menace behind them was unmistakable.

Sara opened her eyes slowly. The first thing she saw was the button-fly on a pair of well-worn, faded jeans. Her gaze traveled down muscular thighs, following long legs to a pair of highly polished cowboy boots.

The kind of boots a ruthless, dangerous outlaw like the Jaguar, the villain in her latest book, wore.

She swallowed, almost afraid to complete her inspection of this stranger who seemed to have popped right out of her computer screen, straight into this larger-than-life, Technicolor nightmare she was having.

Curiosity, however, was a powerful motivator. Reluctantly, her eyes retraced their path, then moved over lean hips, a flat abdomen and an enormous chest, covered in a white T-shirt and a black leather jacket, up to the hard-planed, deeply bronzed face and coal black hair.

Her first impression of the stranger was that of a leashed, carefully controlled jungle cat, the strong, powerful body held in a deceptively relaxed stance, the watchful silver eyes narrowed slivers of light in a darkly tanned face.

"Get lost, buddy. This is between me and the lady,"

growled Roy, his lascivious gaze riveted to Sara's chest.

She was midway through shivering in revulsion when inspiration finally struck. Before she had a chance to talk herself out of it, she sprang out of her chair, one arm still caught in Roy's unrelenting grip.

"Buddy! I'm so glad you made it!" she exclaimed in a high-pitched voice before flinging herself awkwardly into the stranger's arms. She chanced a quick peek at his face, praying that he would follow her lead, but his expression was completely inscrutable.

You'd think strange women flung themselves at him all the time, thought Sara, even as she tightened her one-armed grip on his neck.

"Buddy, honey—" she affected what she hoped was a sufficiently convincing pout "—I've been waiting and waiting for you. I've been ready to, uh, blow this joint for ages!"

The reality of what she was doing and saying was just beginning to catch up with her. She was finding it strangely difficult to breathe, the music was ringing in her ears, and the fact that her heart was lodged somewhere in her throat was making it hard to swallow.

Not to mention that she practically had the stranger in a headlock now.

He, however, seemed totally unfazed as he disengaged himself from her grip and set her aside with little difficulty. "Party's over, friend. Let her go."

"I'll let her go when I'm good and ready," snarled Roy, scowling at the stranger. "And just who the hell are you, anyway? You were in here way before the dame and I didn't see you staking a claim. She's mine now, so back off, you interferin' sonofa—"

"Bitch?" A cold chill skittered through Sara at the stranger's feral smile. "Heard of me, have you?"

Roy seemed startled for a second, then growled in rage and reached for Sara's other arm. His wrist was neatly caught in midair.

"I believe I asked you to keep your hands to yourself." All traces of civility had disappeared from the stranger's voice, leaving it hard and icy. His wintry gray eyes glittered dangerously.

A sensible man would have heeded the warning, but Roy, in the grip of a drunken rage, seemed long past good sense. He dropped Sara's arm and swung wildly at the stranger, who sidestepped the ham-size fist with laughable ease, then aimed a crushing blow that connected loudly with Roy's jaw. It sent him sailing into a nearby table which cracked, then splintered almost exactly in half. The man sitting there jumped out of his chair and collided with a passing waitress, who let out an earsplitting shriek as her tray tipped over. Beer mugs, nachos and barbecued chicken wings went flying, and then all hell broke loose.

Dakota flexed the stinging fingers of his right hand slowly. Damn it, he'd been hoping things wouldn't go this far, that the drunken idiot he'd just laid flat would have enough sense to back off.

And speaking of idiots, he flicked a glance at the woman standing beside him, staring in mute disbelief at Roy's prone body.

She wasn't beautiful like the redhead. Her hair was straight and mousy brown and her face was nothing out of the ordinary. But from what he could see of her body—which was quite a lot in that fire-engine red dress—she seemed to be stacked to the rafters.

And what luscious rafters they were.

The generous curves of her pale white breasts peeked enticingly over the top of a low-slung neckline, and he envisioned them topped by a pair of deliciously rosy nipples. The thought had barely formed in his mind when a slow, throbbing arousal began between his legs.

He stilled, unable to believe what he was thinking and his body's ensuing reaction. This was it! The sign he'd been waiting for since the explosion, the one that signaled recovery after six long months. Damn, but he needed a woman. He tried frantically to spot the red-head over crashing chairs and flying fists, but she had disappeared from the dance floor.

Frustrated, he turned his attention back to the woman in front of him. She was gawking at the chaos around her in openmouthed astonishment, looking like a nun caught in a whorehouse. Then, slowly, she turned to face him. He didn't like the way she was looking at him, with those wide, awestruck chocolate-colored eyes. He stared grimly back at her.

"If you've got any sense at all, you'll hightail it out of here before this crowd decides to get mean." He nodded toward the door, hoping she'd get the message. But she didn't so much as blink, just kept staring at him with those big brown eyes as though he'd suddenly sprouted two wings and a halo.

"Oh, for crissakes!"

He grabbed her small fingers tightly in his and half dragged her across the barroom. As soon as they stepped out the door and into the clean, crisp air outside, he stopped, turned her around and thrust his face just inches from hers. Then he produced a smile guaranteed to send fear slicing through the toughest of battle-trained soldiers of fortune.

"The bait," he drawled, his gaze dropping pointedly to her chest, "is impressive. But before you dangle it, you'd better figure out exactly what kind of fish it's going to attract." He straightened abruptly and released his tight grip on her fingers. "Otherwise, take up a different hobby."

"Who are you?" she whispered.

"Just call me stupid," he muttered and, turning on his heel, strode into the waiting darkness of the parking lot.

Once upon a time, not too long ago, a good, furniture-busting brawl would have been a welcome diversion under any circumstances. But today there was no adrenaline rush, no excitement, no exhilaration. There was only a vague sense of distaste. And a hell of a lot of pain, he thought ruefully, blowing softly on his bruised and burning knuckles. Using his left hand, he dug into his pocket for the keys, unlocked the door to the black pickup truck and climbed in.

So much for a vacation. Until tonight, he'd spent most of his evenings lounging on the deck of the cottage, staring at the stars and listening to the steady rhythm of the waves washing on the shore. In the two weeks he'd been here he'd only ventured into town a couple of times, mostly to stock up on essentials, and he was sure that each time he walked down Main Street, a succession of little old ladies ogled him through the lace curtains on their windows. Maybe they didn't have anything better to do.

How such a boring, uptight little town as Beaver Creek had spawned a hell-raiser like his partner, Loch MacNamara, was a complete mystery to Dakota. No wonder Loch had been driven to seek adventure in Africa.

Dakota rubbed his jaw tiredly. If he were honest with himself, he'd admit that Beaver Creek wasn't the problem. Just as it hadn't been Kinshasa or Nairobi or Dar es Salaam. It wasn't any *place.*

It was him. It was the familiar restlessness again, that nagging, insistent sensation that pulled at him constantly, like an ocean current tugging on a moored dinghy. After the explosion at the mine, he'd spent over a month in the hospital with nothing better to do than think about the fact that if he'd been standing one more foot to the left, he would have ended up being brought out in a body bag, just like Bill and Foster.

Ever since then, the feelings had eaten away at him, elusive, undefined, but always there. They caused him to become increasingly edgy, restive and impatient. He slowly began to drive everyone around him crazy, until Loch finally suggested dryly that he either lock himself up with a woman until he'd gotten the ants out of his pants, or take a vacation.

He'd tried the first and to his frustration, not to mention his partner's shocked disbelief, it hadn't worked. Literally. He was soft and as incapable of fully satisfying a woman as a damn eunuch. The doctor told him that it could have been the trauma of the explosion that caused him to become temporarily impotent. He had tried again a couple of times after that, but the result was the same.

Nothing. Frustrated and, hell yes, scared, he'd packed his gear and flown halfway around the world to Canada to take up Loch's offer of a month at his secluded cottage in rural Ontario. He had two more weeks to get over this ridiculous problem and then he'd be able to go home again. More than anything, he wanted to get back to the Macota, back to work, back to the normalcy of his life before the explosion.

And just when he'd finally been ready to try again with the sexy redhead, Roy and that nitwit woman had screwed it up.

With a fierce scowl, he turned the key in the ignition and eased the truck expertly out of the crowded parking lot. He chanced a glance at the rearview mirror and saw the lone figure standing just where he'd left her, in the pink glow of the neon sign that read Billy Joe's Bar. She wrapped her arms around herself and hunched her shoulders, as if trying to keep the chill of the summer night at bay.

He shook his head in disbelief. What the hell was she waiting for, an encore?

He waited a few seconds, hoping she'd know enough to make herself scarce, but she just stood there, staring down the long, lonely stretch of highway, looking lost and forlorn.

"Oh, hell!" He hit the steering wheel with the palm of his uninjured hand. He was going to have to rescue the woman from her own foolishness.

Wilder, you pick the damnedest times to get a conscience.

Senility, pure and simple. It had to be. He'd never had a chivalrous thought in his life.

"Honey, don't you have a home to go to?"

The deep, rough voice startled Sara, but when she looked up to find the stranger observing her impatiently from a black pickup truck, a wave of relief washed over her.

He hadn't abandoned her after all.

She smiled up at him and decided to answer his stupid question. "Of course I do."

"Then why don't you save everyone a whole lot of grief and head back to it?" His voice was rife with irritation.

Her smile faded. As far as knights in shining armor went, he was a tad on the surly side. But then again, he'd just started a fistfight to rescue her, so maybe he had a right to be a little grumpy.

She decided to give him the benefit of the doubt. "I can't."

"Why the hell not?"

Okay, so grumpy was an understatement. "I don't have a ride."

He leaned over and opened the passenger side door with barely concealed annoyance. "Get in."

His tone had graduated from grumpy to downright rude. Not to mention that the sheer size of him, his unmistakable maleness and those gleaming gray eyes were beginning to unnerve her. "No, thanks, but if you have a cell phone I could use, I'd appreciate it. I need to check on my taxi."

"A cell phone," he repeated.

Then he swore. Sara blinked at the amount of feeling he managed to put into that one little four-letter word.

"I take it that means you, uh, don't have one?"

"Listen, lady, any minute now, that door behind you is going to open up and either Roy or one of his buddies is going to come out here looking for blood. I don't know about you, but I like to give to worthier causes. And if that isn't incentive enough, some other loser might come out here just drunk enough to decide you're to his liking. And in that outfit, he might reckon you're offering. Get the picture?"

Sara bit her lip in indecision. It had been frightening enough to venture out in the midst of strangers tonight, dressed in a skintight red mini that bared parts of her body that no one except she and God had seen since childhood, pretending to be someone she wasn't. Despite the fact that it made her feel naked, she'd taken the dress out of her character closet and put it on, trying to think of it as a stage costume. Stage costume, ha! Just who was she trying to kid? The only costume she needed tonight was a straitjacket.

"Now get in."

She stared at him for a moment, wondering if she ought to trust him when, suddenly, the door of the bar crashed open and two bodies locked in combat came tumbling out, landing practically at her feet.

Maybe trust was overrated, she thought, dodging the rolling bodies and making a mad dash for the pickup. High heels on gravel made running a precarious proposition, but with a little stumbling, she managed. Climbing into a pickup truck in a dress that barely covered her butt was awkward, but she managed that, too. As soon as she closed the door, the stranger put the truck in gear and hit the accelerator.

Suddenly feeling painfully self-conscious, she tried tugging down at the hem of her dress, but that only made it necessary to yank up at the bodice. She was in the middle of yanking for the third time when a strangled oath erupted from the man beside her.

"Can't you sit still?"

"Sorry," she muttered, quickly folding her hands in her lap. "This dress is a bit...drafty."

Without a word, he started to take off his jacket with one hand while the other held the steering wheel steady, then switched hands and offered the jacket to her. "Here, put this on."

She hesitated for a second and then took the jacket. "Thanks."

She struggled into the black leather, well aware that he was watching her every move from the corner of his eye. The jacket was still warm from his body and smelled faintly of a spicy cologne and clean sweat, the mingled scent oddly disturbing, not unlike the man himself.

A tense silence reigned in the cab for a few minutes before he broke it.

"Where to?"

"Lake Henderson. It's in Beaver Creek, just on Highway 7."

"I know it."

"If you're not going that way, you can just drop me off at the phone booth at the next intersection. I can call another taxi."

He flicked her a curious glance. "Is that how you got to Billy Joe's in the first place?"

She nodded. And as soon as she'd walked in, she'd known she couldn't go through with her ludicrous plan, so she'd called another cab and resigned herself to the wait. And while she'd been waiting, Roy had happened.

"And that's how you planned to get yourself home again?"

There was something in his voice that made her stare at him in puzzlement. And when he turned to look at her, she knew exactly what he was thinking. He had a knowing gleam in his eyes that made the burning heat work its way up her neck to the tips of her ears.

"You don't understand," she said quickly.

"Honey, I understand plenty. You were in that bar

tonight hoping to get picked up, only you didn't count on attracting the likes of lover-boy Roy."

"No, you really *don't* understand! I thought he was Joe when I smiled back at him earlier."

"Curiouser and curiouser."

"It's not what you're thinking. Joe is the janitor at the library and I didn't want to be rude so when he smiled at me from across the bar, I smiled back. Only it wasn't Joe, it was Roy."

And if she'd worn her glasses tonight, she could have avoided the whole mortifying mess. But the thick black frames made her look like a nearsighted owl, so she'd left them at home. She had a feeling that if she confessed *that* to him, he'd turn right around and deposit her in Roy's arms with a good riddance, so she kept her mouth shut.

"I think I owe our friend Roy an apology," he drawled.

"Fine. Believe what you want," she muttered. "Just don't stop driving."

"Honey, if I take my hands off this steering wheel, I may just end up strangling you."

Sara's gaze darted automatically to the steering wheel. As they passed under a streetlight, she caught a glimpse of his right hand and gasped.

He sent her an irritated glance. "What's wrong now?"

"Your hand," she said, nodding to his scraped and raw knuckles. "It's bleeding."

"No kidding."

The crack of his fist connecting with Roy's jaw echoed in her mind and she winced involuntarily. "I'm sorry you had to get hurt."

He shrugged. "Don't worry about it."

Despite his nonchalant attitude, a wave of guilt engulfed Sara. It was her fault that he was hurt and bleeding. If she hadn't gone to the bar tonight, if she'd worn her glasses and hadn't smiled at Roy, if she'd been more adamant or maybe even danced just once with him, the stranger wouldn't have had to rescue her. But he had, and now it was up to her to do something to make amends. She couldn't let him go home without at least offering to take care of his hand.

She took a deep breath and said, "Maybe when we get to my place, I can put some ice on it and wrap it up for you. It's the least I can do to thank you."

Dakota glanced sharply at her, wondering exactly what the invitation implied. Either the woman had absolutely no sense of self-preservation whatsoever or she had something more than just playing nurse on her mind. Or maybe she was just plain crazy. At this point, his money was on crazy. "Maybe."

She smiled tentatively at him.

He stared. The smile made her big brown eyes light up from within and her lips curve in the sweetest way, transforming her features from ordinary to radiant. He shook his head and forced himself to drag his eyes from her face back to the road. He needed to concentrate on his driving, for Pete's sake, not on making calf eyes at some nutty woman.

They completed the remainder of the drive in silence, except when she had to give him directions to her house. He pulled into her driveway, stopped the truck outside the cottage, got out and opened the door for her.

As she turned to climb down, his gaze fell for a moment on her smooth, bare legs, exposed to midthigh, before moving slowly back up to her face. She struggled out of his jacket and handed it to him. He took it without a word and tossed it carelessly onto the seat. When he turned back, she was engrossed in trying to pull her dress up and down at the same time.

He studied her for one long moment. She wasn't very tall, but her legs were every bit as sleek and sexy as the redhead's, and her body was a lot more curvy. Voluptuous. He felt again that unmistakable tightening in his groin and nearly groaned out loud. He needed to get away from here, away from the temptation this woman presented, yet some latent masochism on his part compelled him to step closer instead. "Aren't you going to invite me in?"

Her head snapped up and her hands dropped instantly to her sides. "Sure, yes, of course, Mr....Mr...." She laughed nervously. "I don't even know your name."

"Wilder. Dakota Wilder. And you are...?" he asked softly, tipping up her chin with one finger, until she was staring up at him with those wide brown eyes.

"Sara. Sara Matthews," she whispered.

"Well then, Sara Matthews, why don't we skip the first aid. I have a better idea of how you can thank me," he murmured.

He bent his head slowly and lowered his mouth until it was a breath away from hers. He could smell the sweet fragrance of wildflowers on her skin, could feel her warm breath mingling with his. "Say thank you properly, Sara."

When she didn't respond, he laughed softly. "Shy, honey?" he whispered against her lips before gently capturing them in a slow kiss.

Sara closed her eyes and held herself perfectly still. The dangerous renegade from her vivid writer's imagination had somehow, miraculously, come to life and rescued her. And now, to top it all off, he was kissing her.

I've finally flipped my lid, she thought wonderingly. But before she could figure out how or why, her brain switched off the lights, turned over the Closed sign and locked up shop.

A gentle, soothing warmth invaded her belly as his lips moved tenderly over hers, making her body quiver and her knees go weak. She'd never been kissed quite like this before and she'd certainly never felt this strange, giddy, *alive* feeling. She stood, unmoving, unsure of what exactly she ought to be doing to further this fantasy.

"Kiss me back, Sara," he murmured. "Open your mouth and let me in."

She parted her lips automatically at his command and his tongue slid into her mouth. She gasped at the sudden intimacy of his hot tongue roving and swirling inside her mouth, then moaned as she tasted the unique peppermint-and-whiskey flavor of him.

His hands slid down to her hips and pulled her tightly against him, until she could feel every inch of his aroused body pressed against hers. She opened her eyes at the intimate contact, then allowed them to flutter closed again as a languid, sensual heat spread through her body. Her arms snaked around his neck as she submitted to the wonderfully wicked sensations he aroused in her.

Dakota groaned against her lips, cupping the gentle curve of her buttocks and lifting her up until her soft thighs cradled his erection. Her mouth was sweet and intoxicating and her delicious body was making him tight with raw need. He could feel her soft breasts with their hardened nubs grazing lightly against his chest, could feel her heart thundering against his, could feel her submission in the way her body clung to his for support. But he needed more and he needed it now.

"Let's go inside, honey," he whispered.

2

SARA HAULED HIS MOUTH back to hers with a moan of protest, too intent on the hedonistic pleasure flooding through her to pay any attention to his words.

Again, he broke off the kiss, murmuring, "I know, baby, I want it as much as you do."

She opened her eyes and blinked up at him in confusion. "What did you just say?"

"Honey, I like kinky, but I prefer comfortable and I think your bed might be a little more comfortable than your front lawn."

"K-kinky?"

"Kinky," he repeated huskily. "You know—" his finger traced a leisurely path down from the hollow of her throat, leaving a burning trail of heat in its wake "—living out your wildest fantasies." He grazed the tip of her breast and Sara drew in a sharp, ragged breath as a sweet longing pierced through her. "Anything," he drawled, his smoky, desire-filled eyes staring intently into her own, "that turns you on."

It took a few long seconds for his words to penetrate the sensual haze he had woven around her. Oh, Lord, what was she doing? This wasn't some fictional fantasy, this was real! She, who hadn't even looked at an eligible member of the opposite sex for close to two years, was clinging to this strange but oh-so-sexy man like a bloodsucking leech. In a wave of red hot embarrassment, she jumped out of his embrace and stared speechlessly at him.

He stared back for a few tense, silent moments before asking dryly, "I take it you're not into kinky?"

She shook her head, trying desperately to find something to say, but all that came out was a strangled, "I'm sorry."

"I see." With a last, resigned look at her, he turned around and started walking back to the pickup.

"Wait!"

He paused impatiently at the driver's side door.

"Your hand," she explained. "It might still be bleeding."

"Don't worry, honey. I'll live."

THE NEXT MORNING, Sara awoke to the sound of heavy pounding on the front door.

"Oh, go away!" she groaned, burying her head under the covers. It was too early for visitors, especially when she hadn't managed to get more than a wink's worth of sleep all night. Her brain had kept rerunning every second of her surreal encounter with Dakota Wilder.

The covers didn't do much good. In fact, the pounding just became louder, until she couldn't ignore it. She heaved the covers off with a sigh, slipped on her glasses and squinted into the clock radio by the bed. Nine-thirty on a Saturday morning. There was only one person in the world who had the nerve.

She put on her slippers, pulled on her old blue bathrobe and shuffled her way to the front door with a yawn.

"All right, all right, I'm coming already," she grumbled, throwing open the door and making a face at her visitor. "You. I knew it."

"And a good morning to you too, Sara," said the tall, good-looking blonde as she pushed her way in and closed the door behind her.

"Kate, have I ever told you that your eternal cheerfulness at this godforsaken hour of the day makes me sick to my stomach?"

"All the time, hon, but I forgive you. I know what a grouch you are in the morning." Kate patted Sara's cheek on her way to the kitchen and the coffeemaker.

Sara followed her friend and plopped down on a chair. "I could use some of that right now."

"One of those nights, huh?"

"Yes," replied Sara wearily.

"So?"

"So, what?"

Kate wanted to talk and when Kate wanted to talk, there was no stopping her. "So, either you voluntarily tell me about where you went last night after I left here or I abandon you to caffeine withdrawal."

Sara stared at her friend's expectant expression, fighting the urge to howl at the unfairness of it all. Wasn't there anything in this town even vaguely resembling privacy? She'd deliberately decided to go to the farthest of the two bars in the vicinity of Beaver Creek simply because she hadn't wanted to face the questions this morning. It had been an instinctive act of self-preservation on her part; she hadn't wanted anyone to find out if she failed, not even Kate.

"Sara?"

"How did you know?"

"I called about five times last night and your machine kept picking it up. Alex and I were worried."

Well, at least the whole town didn't know. "I'm sorry you were worried."

"So...where did you go?"

"To Billy Joe's," she mumbled and looked up to see Kate staring at her with a mixture of horror and amazement.

"You went to that sleaze joint *alone?*"

"Well, how was I supposed to know it was a sleaze joint?" she asked irritably.

"You could have tried asking! Never mind that, why on earth would you want to go there anyway? No, wait," Kate said, holding out one hand in an imitation of a traffic cop. "Don't tell me. This has to do with your mother's phone call yesterday, doesn't it?"

Sara nodded.

Kate poured two cups of coffee, pulled up a chair and sat down. "All right, start talking."

Once she started, it was hard to stop.

"Okay, let me see if I have this right. You went out last night to see if you could meet a man to bring to your parents' anniversary party, were attacked by a drunk named Roy and rescued by Dakota Wilder, who wears black snakeskin cowboy boots just like the Jaguar and who kissed you passionately enough to make you forget what day of the week it was?"

"Did I say passionately?"

"Yes, you did. And then he drove off, just like that?"

"Yes, thank God. I don't know what I would have done if he'd been like Roy."

"Sure you do. You would have kneed him in the jewels, just like Desiree did to that creep in *March in Madrid....*" Kate trailed off, a strange expression suddenly crossing her face. "Wait just a minute. I'll be right back."

Sara watched, puzzled, as Kate disappeared into the study, then reappeared a few moments later, triumphantly waving a book in front of Sara's face.

"Here it is!"

"What? Here's what?"

"March in Madrid."

"What does *that* have to do with anything?"

"Everything, I think." Kate flipped frantically through the pages until she found what she was looking for. "Here it is."

"Here's *what?*"

"The part where Desiree and McAllister meet at that bar. Do you remember what happens afterward?"

"Of course I remember. I wrote it, didn't I? She ends up seducing him into giving her information about the microchip. What does that have to do with last night?"

Kate clicked her tongue in exasperation. "Don't you see?"

"I hope you're not turning into a nickel-and-dime psychologist, Kate."

"Not to worry. My insights are worth a heck of a lot more than fifteen cents."

Sara shook her head. This was turning into a completely bizarre conversation, but once Kate got started... She decided to play along. "What insights?"

Kate placed the book on the table and gripped Sara's hands tightly. "When I read your books, sometimes I think I don't know you at all. You've been living in Beaver Creek for what, two years? In all that time, you haven't told a single soul except me what you really do for a living. You never go out unless it's to the library for research or to the shooting range or for essentials in town or unless I drag you someplace, kicking and screaming. You crochet in winter, garden in summer, and you're always, always writing. I keep asking myself what kind of a life that is for a twenty-nine-year-old woman. Then I read your books. Spies and secrets, pain and passion, life and death in exotic locations. And I begin to wonder if the person I know is just a shell and if Sara Matthews, the *real* Sara Matthews, is living her life someplace between the covers of a book."

Sara snatched her hands away. "Enough with the melodrama, Kate. I'm a writer. It's what I do. I have a living to make and a deadline to meet, so I sit down in front of the computer and I write, and what I write is fiction. Make-believe. A fantasy. It is *not* real life."

And she had no intention of telling Kate that she'd nearly forgotten as much herself last night. Thank God she'd come to her senses in time!

"No, it's not. And yesterday, I think you finally realized it for yourself. You decided that if Desiree could wear a sexy red dress and go out and get her man, then so could you."

"What's that supposed to mean?"

"It means, my dear, obtuse friend, that your plan worked. You've hooked your fish, now all you have to do is reel him in."

A shudder rippled through Sara at Kate's unfortunate choice of analogy. "No way. Forget the plan. Cut the line and throw away the pole. I don't want any part of it." Then, in disbelief, she added, "And I can't believe you think I have an alter ego problem!"

"What do you mean, you don't want any part of it? The big day is less than a month away! And you're the one who said you were going to show up with a man in tow."

"I know, I know." Sara rubbed her bloodshot eyes

wearily under her glasses. "I never should have agreed to go to that party. It's just... Oh, I don't know what came over me."

"It's called the self-preservation instinct, honey."

"No, it's called stupidity."

She should have said no, the way she had every other year, but when she had heard her mother's voice over the phone yesterday morning, her conscience had kicked in. After all, it was her parents' thirtieth wedding anniversary, and it seemed that, just this once, she should come out of her self-imposed exile and make an appearance. As soon as the yes had popped out of her mouth, her mother had dropped the bombshell that Parker Jackson and his new fiancée were also going to be in attendance. If there was one person in the whole world she never wanted to set eyes on again, it was her ex-fiancé. Of course, if she hadn't been so racked by guilt, she would have seen it coming....

"Well, if I were you, I wouldn't be too hard on myself. Especially after your mother offered to set you up with that nerdy Walt guy just so Parker and what's-her-name wouldn't feel awkward at the party."

Sara nodded her head in bewilderment, still unable to believe what she had done. As soon as her mother had made the offer, something inside had snapped. She opened her mouth and the next thing she knew, her mother was saying how glad she was that Sara had finally found someone on her own and how much she was looking forward to meeting him.

"Don't worry about it, honey." Kate grinned. "You were bound to snap sooner or later. With your parents, I'm surprised it didn't happen sooner."

Sara had to keep herself from smiling and her admonitory "Kate!" didn't come out quite as sternly as it should have.

"Anyway, I think this experience is good for you. You've been hiding yourself in your little fictional world too long. It's time to come out and see the real thing."

"I saw it yesterday and to tell you the truth, I don't think the real world is ready for the real me. Honestly, you should have seen me, Kate. I swear I had the man in a headlock. He must have thought I was a complete idiot."

"You can't hide forever. Some day you're going to have to come out and face reality."

"I'm not ready."

"You just need some time to adjust. And if you're honest with yourself, you'll admit that it was pretty exciting."

Kate's words immediately conjured up the memory of Dakota Wilder's big, hard body pressed against hers, the feel of his warm, firm lips moving slowly on top of her own, and the taste of him when he'd slid his tongue inside her mouth.... "I, uh, don't know what you mean."

"Judging from the shade of red creeping up your face at this very minute, I'd say you know exactly what I mean," said Kate dryly. "And if you're smart, you'll take advantage of his attraction to you."

"It wasn't me he was attracted to. It was some stranger, an act. Maybe you're right, maybe it was Desiree. Besides, it's a moot point. I'll probably never see him again."

"Why not? He's staying right here in town."

An ominous feeling started to churn in Sara's gut. "What do you mean?"

"Exactly what I said. He's in town for at least another couple of weeks."

"What!" Sara jumped out of her chair and stared at Kate, aghast. "Here? In Beaver Creek? How do you know?"

"He's the guy I was telling you about a couple of weeks ago, remember? Alex's cousin Loch's friend."

"You mean the one who was involved in that diamond mine explosion?"

Kate had told her that her husband's cousin, Loch MacNamara, and his partner owned a diamond mine someplace in Africa. Sara had been fascinated by the idea, and she remembered thinking how interesting it would be to meet them both. At the time, her writer's imagination had conjured up two tough, wiry, leather-faced old men. Never in her wildest dreams had she envisioned anyone like the man she had met last night!

"That's the one. Alex told me that he thinks Dakota's been spending too much time alone, so he's planning on taking him out tonight and introducing him around to some of the guys."

"Oh, Lord!" Sara groaned. "Just what I need. A walking, talking reminder of my stupidity." She started to pace frantically back and forth across the kitchen. "What am I going to do, Kate? You know how this town is. If he tells even one person what really happened, the entire episode will probably end up being engraved on my tombstone."

"Now, honey, don't panic."

Sara stopped and took a deep breath. "You're right. There's no point in panicking now. The damage is done."

But if she was very, very lucky he wouldn't remember her, the whole episode would disappear into the mists of time and no one in Beaver Creek would be the wiser.

Except maybe her.

"So, what's the next step?"

Sara looked at her friend blankly. "What next step?"

"In the manhunt."

"The next step is a reality check, and the reality is that this manhunt is a dumb idea. Let's face it, I'm not exactly cut out for that sort of thing."

"Why not?" demanded Kate.

"Because I don't know the first thing about meeting a man and even if I did, I wouldn't be able to go near him without turning into a blithering idiot. God knows, last night was proof enough of that."

"Honey, you're a successful, intelligent woman with a warm heart and a great sense of humor. So what if you're a little shy around strangers? It just means that a man has to persevere, dig a little under the surface to find the hidden treasure."

"Great. Excuse me while I go trade in my fishing pole for a shovel."

"Do it quick. You'll need it for the barbecue this afternoon."

"Is that *this* afternoon?" She'd planned on sitting down and doing some serious writing today so that she could honestly tell her agent that her next book, *July in Jerusalem*, was on schedule.

"Don't you even *think* about making up some lame excuse at the last minute just because Dakota's going to be there," warned Kate. "You're going to come if I have to hog-tie you and piggyback you there myself. Besides, I want you to think seriously about him as a potential candidate. I mean, you've got to admit, he's a perfect match for your mother. Good-looking, sexy, charming—"

"Dangerous..."

Kate grinned. "Like I said, he's perfect. Your mother will never know what hit her."

If Dakota Wilder had the same impact on her mother that he'd had on her last night, Kate was absolutely right. Elizabeth Matthews would never know what hit her. The thought made Sara smile, but her smile faded as another thought occurred to her.

"Even if I did decide he was perfect, what makes you think he'd agree to do it?"

"Page 142."

"Page 142?"

Kate waved *March in Madrid* in front of her face. "If Desiree can do it, so can you."

Sara groaned.

"Just come and check him out, Sara," urged Kate. "You don't have to commit yourself to anything. You don't even have to talk to him if you don't want to."

"Has anyone told you that you're incredibly pushy, Kate?"

"Hey, what can I say? It's a gift."

SARA STOOD in front of Kate's kitchen window and watched the group of men clustered near the barbecue grill. In particular, her gaze focused in on the tall, dark-haired man standing next to Kate's husband Alex.

Everything about him fascinated her. The predatory way he moved, slowly, purposefully, each movement calculated and smoothly controlled. The deliberately casual way he stood, leaning back against the picnic table, his big body held perfectly still, arms crossed, head cocked slightly to the left. The thoughtful way he crouched down to talk to the little girl who brought him a piece of apple pie and the heart-stopping smile and wink he gave her before she went running back to her mother.

"So, what do you think?"

Sara turned her attention back to the melon she was supposed to be slicing for the fruit tray. She wasn't sure she liked the note of satisfaction she'd heard in Kate's voice.

"Looks like rain," she answered blandly.

"If I wanted a weather update, I'd have turned on the radio. Talk to me."

"Okay, so you were right. He's perfect," admitted Sara grudgingly.

If she'd had any reservations about Dakota Wilder, seeing him in action this afternoon had dispelled them. The lethal charm she'd witnessed just before he'd kissed her last night had been in plenty of evidence. That, along with his dark, dangerous good looks and mysterious background had guaranteed him a captivated audience, from cranky old Mrs. Nelson to Kate's fifteen-year-old nephew, Jeff.

Kate grabbed a slice of melon and bit into it. "Hey, don't sound so thrilled about it."

"Kate, it's not going to work."

"What's not going to work?"

"This...this whole manhunt-seduction thing."

"Why? What happened? Did you talk to him? What did he say?"

"Well, no, I didn't exactly talk to him." Although she'd been watching him all afternoon, she'd been careful to keep her distance. Every time he'd come within twenty feet of her, she'd tried to sneak away, undetected. She'd nearly been cornered around the condiment table once, but he'd walked right past without recognizing her.

And that was the problem.

"So what exactly *did* you do?"

"I observed him and I...and...closely. I observed him closely."

Kate picked up some slices of melon and began arranging them on a platter. "Oh, Sara, you're such a coward!"

"So, what's your point?"

"Why haven't you approached him yet?"

Sara put down her knife in exasperation. "Because he didn't recognize me! What did you want me to do? Go up to him, thrust out my hand and say, 'Hi, remember me? I'm the blithering bimbo you rescued last night.'"

"It's original."

"Kate, pay attention."

Kate put the slices of melon down with a sigh and turned to face Sara. "What?"

"He didn't recognize me. He didn't look twice. He didn't even look once. He couldn't possibly have been attracted to me last night. It was the dress and that whole Desiree thing."

"Honey, did you look at yourself in the mirror before you left the house this afternoon?"

Sara opened her mouth to say yes, then snapped it shut and frowned instead. Well, she'd looked at her face in the bathroom mirror while she'd brushed her teeth this morning, but she had a feeling that wasn't what Kate meant. She had to admit that she'd fallen out of the habit of looking in the mirror since she'd moved to Beaver Creek. Living alone and working from home meant that she didn't have to worry about how she looked; no one but Kate ever visited her anyway. And when she went out, she normally just threw on her sweats or an old pair of jeans.

Except for last night.

Last night she'd spent a long, long time in front of that mirror.

"I take it that's a no," said Kate dryly.

"I didn't really have time. I was working until you called and then—"

"—you grabbed your purse and rushed out of the house without thinking because you were late," concluded Kate.

"Well, you said to hurry," said Sara defensively.

Kate rolled her eyes. "I bet your own mother wouldn't recognize you in this getup, so what makes you think that a perfect stranger, a *man* at that, who saw you in a red minidress for a couple of hours last night, would?"

Sara glanced down at her worn-out jeans and oversized T-shirt and grimaced. "Okay, point taken. But I'm not going around wearing Desiree's clothes."

"Trust me, honey, no man is worth that much trouble. Let's just say that a few minutes in front of a mirror before you leave the house wouldn't hurt. Now, about this manhunt thing—"

"Kate dear, is the fruit ready?" Mrs. MacNamara, Kate's mother-in-law, popped her head into the kitchen, saving Sara the trouble of sticking the paring knife into her friend's ribs.

"Sara!" The old lady's blue eyes lit up and she hurried over to give Sara a big hug.

"Hi, Mrs. Mac."

"Where have you been hiding yourself? I haven't

seen you at the store since last week." She peered up at Sara in concern. "Have you been ill, dear?"

Sara smiled. Mrs. MacNamara, the proud owner of Beaver Creek's only grocery and convenience store, was a sweetheart. "No, ma'am. I've been busy with work."

Mrs. MacNamara frowned. "Mr. Martin at the post office said you received three large packages last week. More books to edit?"

Sara forced herself to keep her smile in place and nod. After two years of practice, she'd become at whole lot better at lying to the good people of Beaver Creek about what she did for a living. The only person who knew she was L. A. Michaels, the *New York Times* best-selling author of spy novels, was Kate and she'd been sworn to secrecy.

As far as the rest of the town was concerned, she was a freelance editor. It was the perfect way to explain what she did all day at home and why she received and sent so many packages to a publishing house in New York. And although the ruse was necessary in a town where everyone minded everyone else's business, no matter how long she practiced, she could never get rid of the guilt that gnawed at her insides every time she told the lie. Especially to Mrs. MacNamara, who made it no secret that she was a die-hard fan of L. A. Michaels.

Mrs. MacNamara patted Sara on the arm. "Well, don't work too hard, dear," she said, picking up the fruit tray and walking to the door. "And try not to let our Katie give you too hard a time."

Kate sent her mother-in-law's retreating back a look of affectionate exasperation. "Do I ever give you a hard time?"

"It's a gift, remember?" Sara quipped as she rinsed her hands under the tap. "Listen, I have to run." She grabbed her purse from the counter and gave Kate a hug.

"Wait a minute! What about the manhunt? Are you going to do it or not?"

"I don't know. I'll think about it. Right now I've got a hero at home waiting to be rescued."

THE EXPLOSION of thunder startled Sara just enough for her fingers, tapping against her desk, to lose their rhythm. Straightening in her chair, she turned her attention back from the inky darkness outside the window of her study to the gray glare of her computer screen. It had been seven hours since she'd returned from Kate's house, and she was still trying to work out exactly how McAllister was going to escape the Turkish prison and catch up with the Jaguar.

And he, she decided, was the whole problem. The dark, dangerous renegade had captured her imagination and completely overshadowed her hero. The man occupying most of her thoughts now wasn't Jonathan McAllister, ordinary-Joe-turned-master-spy. That honor belonged to a certain charcoal-haired, silver-eyed stranger who was infinitely more dangerous than the protagonist of her latest novel. Dangerous because he was all too real, not just a figment of her imagination that she could manipulate according to whim. As a result, she'd written the grand total of exactly one sentence in the past seven hours. She'd fiddled with it and revised it countless times before deleting it altogether.

Usually, she had no problem writing brash, daring Jon into and out of the most incredible scrapes, but it seemed that she was going to have to resort to more drastic measures today. Slowly, she rose, pulled off her glasses and glared at the screen.

"So it's come to this, has it, Jon?"

The monitor glared back.

"You're going to lie there and play dead, just like you did with that darned assassin in *January in Johannesburg*, and let the Jaguar get the best of you?" she gibed in disgust. "Sure, the Jaguar is clever and dynamic and managed to outsmart you and get Desiree, but there are still six chapters to go! You've been down before, but you've always managed to come out on top. You have to. You're the hero. Now get up and act like one." She sat back down, hoping that her little pep talk would either encourage or shame Jon into telling her what happened next. It didn't.

"All right, McAllister, you leave me no other choice."

Coolly, with stiff, deliberate movements, she walked from her study to the closet in the front hall. She opened the door slowly and reached up to retrieve a nondescript hatbox and an old dun-colored trench coat. Kneeling on the floor, she uncovered the box, reverently lifted out a battered black fedora and carefully placed it on top of her head, adjusting it to just the right angle. Then she slipped the trench coat on over her cotton nightgown, belted it tightly and made for the stereo in the study. A little bit of fiddling and the funky sounds of Aretha Franklin belting out "R-E-S-P-E-C-T" flooded the house. With a satisfied sigh she lay down on the black leather love seat and closed her eyes. The soothing ritual, one she'd practiced every day while writing her first two books, was comfortingly familiar. Now all she had to do was wait.

And wait. And wait some more. Through six playbacks of Aretha's pleas for respect. Finally, fed up, she jackknifed into a sitting position and cursed.

"Damn you, Jonathan McAllister, for a stubborn jackass and a coward to boot!"

She got up and stomped to the kitchen. There was only one thing that had never let her down this close to a self-imposed deadline before. White chocolate chip ice cream. That was the ticket. She could already feel the cold, creamy confection sliding down her throat. She opened the freezer in slow anticipation and stopped short when she saw the empty spot where she usually kept the ice cream.

And then she remembered throwing the carton into the trash not four days ago. Frantically, she searched the rest of the freezer, hoping to find a long-forgotten container hidden behind the lamb chops or something, but to no avail. Panic began to set in. If she didn't get some, she'd never be able to finish the book. Jon had never been this troublesome before and she was going to need all the help she could get in bringing him around. She needed ice cream and she needed it now.

Grabbing her purse from the front hallway, she slipped on a pair of sneakers and raced out the front door.

Ten minutes later, she was running through the slashing rain, making blindly for the flashing red neon sign in the window of MacNamara's Grocery and Convenience store. She dashed through the door just as another bolt of lightning streaked across the black sky, followed closely by a deafening crack of thunder.

"Sara!" exclaimed Mrs. MacNamara from behind the counter. "Have you run out again?"

"I'm afraid so, Mrs. Mac," she said ruefully, trying to wipe her glasses dry with an already damp tissue.

"Oh dear, and in such horrible weather, too. Why look at you, you're drenched."

Sara tried unsuccessfully to shake the moisture from her trench coat. The water had already soaked through to her nightgown; she could feel it sticking uncomfortably to her body. Despite Kate's dire warning this afternoon, Sara hadn't bothered to change because it was past midnight and nobody in their right mind would be out, especially in weather like this.

Unless, of course, they were occasionally plagued with bizarre cravings for ice cream.

"Well, go on to the back, dear. I think we have a couple of containers left."

"Thanks, Mrs. Mac."

As she walked far to the back of the store, Sara heard the chimes which signaled the arrival of another customer. Not wanting to be seen by whoever it was, she hurried to the freezer section, shivering as the cold started to seep through her wet clothes.

DAKOTA STRODE into the well-lit store, accompanied by a gust of warm wind and cool rain.

"Hi, darlin'," he greeted the old woman at the counter, flashing her a grin as he swiped a leather-clad arm across a face dripping with rainwater.

A faint blush touched Mrs. MacNamara's lined cheeks, but she gave him a stern look. "What are you doing out in weather like this, young man?" she asked.

"Taking a shower with my clothes on," he teased. "Care to join me?"

"Don't you even think about using your glib tongue on me, Dakota Wilder. I know when I'm being sweet-talked."

"Why, honey, how would a sweet young thing like you learn about stuff like that?"

"Huh!" scoffed Mrs. MacNamara. "I learned everything I needed to know from spending time with that rascal nephew of mine."

Dakota's grin faltered slightly. Sometimes, he was sure that Loch's stories about summers with his Aunt Martha and cousin Alex had been the only things that had kept them sane in that hellhole of an Angolan prison. For the thousandth time, he thanked God for the woman who had raised his friend.

"Now, young man, what can I get for you?"

He didn't know. He couldn't say why he'd come in here. Except that he'd been on his way back to the cottage after spending the evening with Alex and the guys at the Honky Tonk and the restlessness had begun to haunt him again. When he'd seen the flashing neon light in front of the store from his truck, he'd pulled in on impulse. Perhaps he didn't want to be alone again tonight and he knew he could count on Mrs. MacNamara to supply an unending stream of chatter to keep him occupied, at least for a little while.

"I came back for the sequel to that book you recommended yesterday."

He winced inwardly at the lie. The book she'd talked him into buying was still sitting on his coffee table, where he'd tossed it after coming home yesterday.

Mrs. MacNamara beamed up at him. "Didn't I say you were going to like it?"

"Yes, ma'am."

"You're in luck, then. I think there are a few copies of his latest left. Come on, I'll show you. Now that I've got you hooked," she commented thoughtfully, "I've got to work harder on that Sara. She's the only one in this town who isn't addicted to L. A. Michaels."

His head jerked up involuntarily at the mention of Sara's name.

"Lord knows I've tried to get her to read them, but she just isn't interested." Mrs. MacNamara began searching energetically through the rack of paperbacks. "She's a sweet girl, our Sara. Reminds me of a quiet little mouse sometimes. She's been living at that cottage of hers for the past two years almost like a hermit. Too busy editing those books of hers and far too young to be left alone if you ask me. It's just not right, a pretty little thing like her. What she needs is a nice young man to take some interest in her." She sighed over a romance novel and tucked it into her pocket before continuing her search. "Only thing is, the pickings are pretty slim around here. Do you know of any eligible bachelors, Dakota?"

"No!" His reply came out more sharply than he'd intended.

Mrs. MacNamara turned and peered questioningly up at him.

He shifted uncomfortably. "Africa is a long way to go to meet anyone I know."

A strange gleam entered the old lady's blue eyes. "Have you met our Sara?"

"We haven't been formally introduced, if that's what you mean," he hedged.

"Well, why don't you go on to the back and *formally* introduce yourself," Mrs. MacNamara suggested as she thrust the book at him.

He pocketed it absently and stared thoughtfully at the back of the store. "I think I might just do that, ma'am."

3

CHOCOLATE CHERRY MINT. Sara frowned at the last remaining container of ice cream in the freezer. It was a flavor she'd never tried before and, to be quite honest, it didn't sound terribly appetizing, but ice cream was ice cream and when the craving struck, she couldn't afford to be picky. With a shrug, she opened the freezer and reached in for it.

"Midnight cravings, sweetie?" The deep, soft voice was a seductive whisper in her ear.

She gasped and straightened abruptly, colliding backward into a very hard, muscular chest. The container slipped out of her suddenly nerveless fingers. His arms came around her and deftly rescued the ice cream before it could hit the ground at her feet.

She tried to remain motionless in his embrace, but her heart was hammering in her chest at an alarming rate and she found it was hard to breathe. Instead of moving away, he leaned forward deliberately, until she felt his warm breath at her nape and the heat of his body warming her back and legs. He took his sweet time turning the container around in his large, darkly tanned fingers and scanning the label.

"Chocolate cherry mint," he mused. "Interesting choice."

"There wasn't much. Choice I mean," she said, her voice coming out in an awkward croak.

"Is this the last container? Maybe we'll have to share it, hmm?"

Sara gulped at the suggestiveness of his tone. "No, you go ahead and enjoy it."

He drew back slowly and replaced the ice cream in the freezer. "Scared, Sara?" he taunted softly.

She squeezed her eyes shut. Scared? Uh-uh. *Terrified* was a much better word for what she was feeling. Terrified that she was too weak to resist the temptation that Dakota Wilder, with his sexy smile and wicked charm, offered. There was a reckless part of her that wanted to throw caution to the wind and give in to the temptation to be Desiree, to be the woman he wanted, consequences be damned. But a bigger part of her also knew that consequences had to be faced and that, for a woman like her, they were always painful. Hadn't she learned her lesson from Parker?

"Isn't that why you were running from me this afternoon?"

She spun around at his smoothly voiced question and stared into his amused gray eyes in amazement.

"But I wasn't... How did you know it was me?"

"It would be impossible to mistake those big brown eyes of yours, even hidden behind those glasses. And if you weren't running, what exactly were you doing?"

The familiar heat began to work its way up her face. She'd been spying on him, that's what. But she could hardly come right out and admit that to him. Instead, she asked, "Why did you let me think that you didn't recognize me?"

"You were having such a good time trying to avoid me, I decided not to spoil your fun. I know how...frustrating it is to be thwarted in the middle of an amusing game."

Sara licked her lips nervously. Was it just her imagination or was it suddenly too hot in here? "I have to go now. Excuse me."

Dakota found his gaze straying involuntarily to her soft, moist mouth just in time to catch sight of that pink tongue as it darted out to run lightly over her full lower lip. His stomach muscles clenched at the seemingly innocent yet oddly erotic gesture and he reached out to trace a finger over the glistening trail her tongue had left behind. He heard her soft gasp and saw her eyes widen incredulously as his finger made contact with the sensitive pink flesh.

"Running again?" he asked huskily, letting his finger trail gently down her jaw and the delicate line of her throat. He stopped to feel the mad thudding of her pulse, then continued down the warm, slightly damp skin until he encountered white cotton.

Sara felt his touch burn a fiery path down her skin and she closed her eyes to try to block it out. Instead, she found herself savoring the feel of his finger against her flesh more fully. How could such simple contact generate so much heat, so much need? The feelings his kiss had aroused in her the previous night came tumbling back. Her breath started to come in shallow gasps, a strange, queasy warmth gathered in the pit of her stomach and her knees actually felt weak. She wanted so much to feel his hot mouth moving over hers, his hard length pressed against her....

"This time you won't get away so easily, sweet Sara."

She opened her eyes at the sensual promise in his words, only to encounter his smoldering gray gaze.

"I wonder which part you're playing now. Is it this afternoon's Victorian virgin or last night's sexy siren?"

His fingers slid down to the belt of her trench coat and deftly unknotted it, then slowly parted the material. Sara didn't resist. She couldn't. All she could do was stare helplessly into those hypnotic eyes.

Dakota tore his gaze from hers and let it slide down to the wet cotton that clung so lovingly to the generous curves of her breasts. The nipples burgeoned into tight peaks under his intense scrutiny. Desire slammed into him with the force of a freight train at full speed and he felt his own arousal straining against his jeans.

"A little of both, I think," he murmured throatily. "The white cotton nightgown is very Victorian, but the body underneath is definitely sexy." He tilted his head consideringly. "Somehow, it's not quite what I pictured you wearing to bed."

Her eyes were dark and dazed as she stared up at him. "I wasn't in bed."

"Now that raises some interesting possibilities, wouldn't you say?"

"We shouldn't be doing this," she said breathlessly, even as her body leaned towards him. "Mrs. Mac...she might see."

"I've only looked at you, Sara, and you're already aroused," he whispered provocatively in her ear, ignoring her misgivings. "You can't hide it from me, I can see it through this tent you call a nightgown. Your nipples are hard and aching and I haven't even touched you there yet. I wonder what would happen if I did? If I took you into my mouth?"

She whimpered softly at the erotic images his words evoked in her mind and the accompanying heat that flooded her body. "Why...why are you doing this?"

"For the same reason you are. Because it's wicked and sexy and exciting...and because you like it." He smiled slowly before pulling out the ice cream and closing her fingers around the frozen container. "Here, I think you need this more than I do."

And then, as suddenly as he'd arrived, he was gone.

DAKOTA CLIMBED into the truck, leaned his head back and squeezed his eyes tightly shut. The pungent aroma of wet leather filled the cab, but it didn't erase the scent of wildflowers that clung to his memory. Cold rainwater trickled down his collar, yet it didn't extinguish the fire Sara had ignited inside him.

The dratted woman had done it to him again. Or rather, he'd done it to himself. All he'd intended to do tonight was head on back to the cottage and try to get some sleep. He'd spent the entire evening playing pool and trying not to think about anything more strenuous than which ball to pocket next.

But every once in a while, a picture of Sara Matthews and her big brown eyes had flashed into his mind. He kept picturing how she'd looked this afternoon at the barbecue in that oversize T-shirt and those scruffy old jeans. Her hair had been caught up in a single braid, her skin had been scrubbed clean of makeup and she'd been sporting the ugliest pair of glasses he'd ever seen.

And as soon as he'd seen her, he'd wanted her.

Just the knowledge that he *could* want a woman had been a sweet agony for him. He'd been up all last night, tossing and turning in frustration. After being denied the pleasure of a woman in bed for six months, it had been damn near torture for his body to be aroused to such an extent and then be refused the ultimate satisfaction. But he had never bedded an unwilling woman in his life and he wasn't about to start now. If he had learned anything during those hellish years in Angola, it was self-control.

Only his self-control wasn't doing him much good now. He was uncomfortably aroused, and it was all his own fault. For some reason, when Mrs. MacNamara had told him that "sweet" little Sara was in the back of the store, he'd been compelled to see her again.

He frowned in the dark confines of the pickup. Mrs. MacNamara had described Sara Matthews as a mouse, but she'd been anything but mouselike last night when he'd kissed her and she certainly hadn't been a few minutes ago. On the other hand, at the barbecue he'd noticed that she'd talked mostly with the women, and she'd done everything but jump into the potato salad to avoid him.

So who was the real Sara Matthews? The shy little hermit or the tease in the red hot mini? And why did he give a damn anyway?

Sara took off her glasses, pinched the bridge of her nose and squeezed her eyes shut. She was exhausted, having spent the past eight hours trying to keep her fingers moving at a fast enough rate to capture the story her imagination kept spitting out. Needless to say, the chocolate cherry mint ice cream had worked wonders.

And now that inspiration had worn off and exhaustion had set in, she was having trouble trying to put the thought of last night's encounter with Dakota Wilder out of her mind. The images kept chasing themselves around in her head. The feel of his hard, warm body against hers, the touch of his finger against her breast, the provocative eroticism of his words...

He'd left her weak-kneed and wanton in the store

last night and it had taken her five minutes of pressing the cold container of ice cream to her forehead before she'd been able to walk out of there. And that's when she'd realized how absurd it was to even *think* that she could seduce him into helping her. Before she even had an opportunity to flutter her lashes, he'd probably be zipping up his pants and saying, "Thank you, ma'am."

The man was too sexy, too intimidating, and too darn much for her to handle!

Which was why she was going to call her mother this very morning and unconfirm her attendance at the party. Her mother would be disappointed of course, but that was nothing new.

Sighing, she saved the night's work on the hard drive and a floppy, turned off the computer, poured herself a glass of iced tea in the kitchen, and picked up the receiver.

"YOU WHAT?"

"You know me, dear," said Mrs. Matthews happily. "I couldn't possibly keep such good news to myself."

Sara gripped the receiver tightly as she saw all her hopes of ending this fiasco disappear with her mother's cheerful confession. "You...haven't told anyone else, have you?"

"Don't be silly, darling! I had to tell Parker and Anne that everything's been taken care of and that they don't have to worry about any awkward scenes. Anne was relieved, but Parker didn't seem at all worried. He was quite certain that you'd be reasonable about this entire affair."

Sara felt the beginnings of a headache pressing at her temples.

"And a couple of the girls asked if you were going to be at the party, so naturally I had to tell them."

Naturally. Sara groaned inwardly. This was one contingency she hadn't anticipated.

"Have you been shopping yet? Why don't you come down next weekend and we'll see if we can't get you something suitable. Your father says he'll pay for it. I know you can't possibly afford a decent outfit from the money you make with your scribbling. Really, darling, I can't imagine why you persist with that childish nonsense. Why don't you just come home and..."

Let me fix you up with that nice Ackerman boy.

Sara closed her eyes and started counting backward from one million. She'd given up trying to explain to her parents about her choice of profession a long time ago. They'd never understood the fact that her writing was the one area of her life where she didn't have to worry about being inadequate. People liked her stories, and they didn't care if she couldn't waltz or carry on an inane conversation or blow a year's salary in one shopping trip. It was the one place where she was accepted unconditionally, where she could be who she wanted to be, whether it was a sexy seductress or an adventurous master spy, without having to face the disastrous consequences afterward. No one got hurt and she made a damn good living from her fantasies, despite what her parents believed. But Elizabeth Matthews had never understood how a woman could want anything more from life than to be a socialite wife, with its accompanying powers and privileges, and Sara was tired of explaining.

"Sara? For heaven's sake, try to pay attention."

"I'm sorry, Mother. I can't make it this weekend. I'll get Kate to help me choose something."

A small, disapproving silence stretched over the line before her mother asked, "Was there a special reason why you called, dear?"

"Not really. I...I just wanted to tell you how much my, um, young man is looking forward to meeting you and Daddy," she lied weakly.

"You know," said Mrs. Matthews thoughtfully, "you haven't told us his name yet."

"Haven't I? Why it's... Oh dear, is that the doorbell? Listen, Mother, I really have to run now. The man who's installing my, er, Persian rug is here. Tell Daddy I sent my love."

"But—"

"Goodbye, Mother." Sara dropped the receiver onto its cradle as though it were a live snake, then dropped her aching head into her hands.

SARA WALKED to the entrance of the bar, which consisted of a set of wooden double doors and the requisite neon sign that simply read The Honky Tonk. She wasn't quite sure what to expect. Kate and Alex had tried to convince her to come out here with them a few times, and now she regretted not accepting the invitation. She only hoped that it wasn't anything like Billy Joe's.

As she stared at the imposing set of doors, she wondered how it was possible for an ephemeral madness to transform itself into this insane...*manhunt.* She winced inwardly at the deliberately calculating sound of the word, but how else could she describe it? She really *was* on a manhunt, and the man she needed to find was Dakota Wilder.

Two minutes after she'd learned that her mother had told everyone in the known universe that Sara was bringing a date to the party, she'd finally accepted the inevitable.

Kate was right.

Dakota Wilder was her best and only hope for finding a date for that party. However, there was absolutely no way she was going to attempt to seduce him into accompanying her. Instead, she'd decided to take the calm, rational approach: she was going to explain the situation to him, terrified woman to dangerous man, and politely ask him to be her date. And if that didn't work, maybe *then* she'd consider squeezing herself back into that red dress and digging up some long-forgotten reserve of feminine wiles. Whatever it took, she was going to do. If she didn't, her mother would never forgive her for humiliating the family yet again.

Besides, there was an issue of personal dignity involved here now. She'd let Parker run her out of town once before and she'd been hiding like a frightened little rabbit in its warren for the past two years, but she'd be damned if she'd back out of going to that party now. She would not give Parker the satisfaction of thinking that she was still nursing a broken heart over him, and she would show up at her parents' house with a date if it killed her.

Which, with her track record, was a distinct possibility.

Sara sent up a quick little prayer before hauling one of the massive doors open. The first thing that hit her was a wall of live music, followed by raucous laughter. She managed to avoid tripping over the threshold, but only barely because just then a large man walked by, smiled and tipped his Stetson at her. Sara stared at him, wide-eyed, then caught herself and gave him a smile in return.

She walked in and swept her gaze covertly over the interior, hoping to find an empty table near the door, but they were all taken, except for a couple of seats at the bar.

Taking a deep breath and wiping her moist palms down the sides of her only pair of decent jeans, she walked to the nearest bar stool and perched on the very edge.

"Haven't seen you around here before. You new?" asked a gravelly, English-accented voice.

Sara's head snapped up at the question. She was met with a pair of black eyes set in the meanest looking face she had ever seen. The man was completely bald with large ears and a hideous, puckered white scar running right from the edge of one pierced ear to his mouth. He was practically breathing in her face as he leaned across the bar. She gulped.

"Yes." Her answer came out as a terrified whisper, but it seemed to satisfy the giant in front of her because he nodded sagely and moved back. He straightened, revealing more of his incredible person, and her mouth nearly dropped open. The man was huge, probably six and a half feet tall and half as wide, with great slabs of muscle that were clearly visible through his black T-shirt.

"What'll you have, then?"

She stared at him, uncomprehending, for a few seconds before it dawned on her that he was the bartender. "Maybe some iced tea?"

"Gotcha, luv. A Long Island iced tea coming right up."

"Just a plain iced…" But he'd already moved away to mix her drink and she took the opportunity to give herself a pep talk.

Calm down, get a grip, relax. Perhaps a drink wasn't such a bad idea. She needed something to take the edge off her nervousness.

Having talked herself into a few sips, she allowed herself to turn slightly in her stool and take stock of her surroundings. The place was cozy, small and shabby, and lacking the sleek, sophisticated surfaces that characterized Billy Joe's. There were fewer tables available and the bar itself was smaller, but the dance floor was just as large and the live band—the Honkers according to the logo on their drums—was better than a jukebox.

Obviously, the patrons thought so, too. The dance floor was crowded with a lively selection of people, men sporting Stetsons and cowboy boots, women wearing long denim skirts or jeans paired with colorful blouses. The clientele here was different from Billy Joe's, a little older and more friendly by the looks of it. Sara stared wistfully at them, wishing she had the nerve to get out there and just let herself go like that. At least she was appropriately dressed, she thought, looking down in relief at her jeans and the pink tank top with the oversize cotton shirt knotted at her waist.

"There you go, luv." The giant placed a tall, frosted glass in front of her. "One iced tea for the lovely lady."

She smiled shyly at him. "Thank you."

He responded with a friendly grin and she thought maybe he wasn't quite so frightening after all. She seized the glass and sipped cautiously, but it didn't taste much different from regular iced tea.

"Mmm. Lovely," she complimented as the cool, soothing blend slid down her throat. She took a couple of quick swallows, finding herself thirstier than she'd thought.

"Mind how you go, sweets."

"Don't worry, I won't choke or anything," she assured him, but put the glass down anyway. She felt better already, calmer and less on edge.

"That's better. Now you look less like you're about to kick off from fright," he said with considerable satisfaction. "Don't worry, luv, I ain't half as bad as I look."

"Oh no, I didn't mean to give you that impression, Mr....?"

"That's Jacko. Just plain Jacko."

She sipped her drink. "I'm Sara. Sara Matthews."

"A right pleasure it is, Sara." Jacko held out a hand that engulfed her own small one, and broke into a grin as she tried not to gape at his huge fist. Chuckling, he excused himself as another customer claimed his attention.

She had finished her drink by the time he came back and felt pleasantly relaxed, more so than she could ever recall being in the company of strangers. This place was nice and it wasn't nearly as nerve-racking as she had expected. Perhaps she would make a habit of coming here. She thought of how surprised Kate would be and giggled.

"Now then, Sara luv, what brings you here tonight?" asked Jacko, wiping his hands on a towel.

Sara frowned at this reminder of exactly why she was here. "I'm looking for a man."

"Well you've come to the right place then. Anyone in particular or will any old bloke do?"

"Oh, no." She shook her head solemnly. "It has to be Wilder."

"I see."

"I knew you would, Jacko. You know, this is a real

nice place. The people are friendly and the music is nice. Not like Billy Joe's.''

"Billy Joe's? You've been there?" He shook his head sadly. "Why, that place is a right meat market. No place for a lady like yourself."

She nodded at his superior understanding of the situation.

"You can relax here. Good old Jacko'll be taking care of you now."

"You're a prince, Jacko."

"Aye, that I am. Look, luv, why don't you have another drink while you're waiting."

It was an excellent suggestion. If one drink could make her feel this good, two had to be even better. "Maybe I will." She held out her empty glass to Jacko and gave him a dazzling smile.

He stepped back as if he'd been socked in the gut and murmured an absent, "Be right back."

Halfway through her second drink, Sara was pleasantly surprised. It seemed that Jacko's magic iced teas had the ability to bypass that annoying quirk in her makeup that usually garbled the messages her brain sent to her body. Tonight she felt as if she could do and say anything she wanted and it would come out how it was supposed to. She wasn't blithering and she knew that her limbs weren't going to be awkward and clumsy when she stood up. In fact, she felt gloriously free and pleasantly buzzed and the beat of the music made her long to get up and move.

She sighed. "Oh, Jacko, I love this music! I only wish I could get out on that dance floor."

"What's stopping you, luv?"

Sara propped her elbow on the bar and dropped her chin onto her hand. "I'm a terrible dancer. Honestly.

My father says a man has to wear steel-toed boots if he doesn't want to end up on crutches."

"Poppycock! Why, you've got the look of a real mover and shaker, see if you don't," retorted Jacko, insulted on her behalf.

She sat up in excitement. "Do you really think so?"

"I'll be a bloomin' teetotaler if you ain't."

Her shoulders slumped again as another thought struck her. "Great, now all I need is a partner."

"Don't you worry your head about that, luv. Jacko'll fix you up right and tight." He searched over her shoulder and nodded his head at someone and the next thing she knew, a nice-looking man in a black Stetson was asking her to dance. She accepted eagerly and jumped off her stool. The room spun a little when she stood up and the nice man had to steady her.

"Whoa there, sweetheart. Take it easy," he said, laughing.

"There just might be more to Jacko's iced teas than I thought," she muttered, then smiled at him. It was his turn to stumble a little before he smiled back and led her to the dance floor. At first she was a little nervous when he placed one hand on her waist and took her hand in the other, especially when she remembered how much her father hated to dance with her.

"Ready, darlin'?" her partner asked.

She took a deep breath and nodded as he twirled her around. She stood stiff and unyielding in his arms for a few minutes and tripped a couple of times before he told her to relax. She took his advice and started to get the hang of it.

"That's it, darlin'. You just keep movin' and let Evan do all the thinkin'."

And suddenly, she knew she was doing it. She could

feel the rhythm of the music pounding in her blood, could feel her feet flying of their own accord, and she tipped back her head and laughed.

"I'm doing it, Evan! I'm dancing!"

"You sure are, darlin'."

DAKOTA LEANED over the table and adjusted the cue a fraction of an inch before giving it a slight nudge, just enough to put the last ball into the corner pocket. A chorus of loud groans echoed around the dingy, smoke-filled room at this accomplishment.

He straightened up and took a long swig from his half-empty bottle of beer. "Well, boys, that's it."

"Come on, Wilder, give us a break, will ya?" groaned Ace. "The least you could do is let us have a crack at it once."

"It's all yours, Ace. Thanks for the beer," he said and walked out the door connecting the pool room with the bar itself. The music, which had been a respectable noise in the pool room, blasted him full force as he made his way to the bar. He motioned the bartender, who approached him at a leisurely pace.

"What'll it be, mate?"

"The usual, Jacko."

He took a swallow as soon as the big man placed the whiskey in front of him, then rubbed the back of his neck tiredly. Tonight he'd finally come to the conclusion that he'd run halfway around the world in an effort to get away from the persistent feelings of dissatisfaction he'd been experiencing lately, and all for nothing. No matter where he went, they followed. He was tired of living with them and he was tired of running from them. All he wanted was to go back to the peace of his life before the explosion. He'd been content then, with his work and his friends. If only he could get past this damn impotence, he'd be able to go back home to the Macota, back to the uncomplicated life he'd made for himself there.

"What's up, Wilder? You're looking a mite peaky tonight."

Dakota looked up in surprise, meeting the bartender's sharp black eyes, and raked his hands through his hair in frustration. "You ever felt restless, Jacko? Like there's nothing more out there for you?"

The bartender stared into space and rubbed his stubbly jaw for a few seconds before answering. "Once. Just after I left the navy. I'd traveled all over the world, seen everything I wanted to see, done everything a man ain't supposed to admit he's done. Didn't think I'd ever get used to being on land again, so I went around drinking myself into a right stupor and raising more hell than what's good for a body. Of course, that was before I met the missus."

Dakota nearly choked on his drink. "The missus?"

A beauteous smile lit up Jacko's ugly face. "Aye, my wife's an angel sent from heaven, she is. Turned my life around good and proper-like. We've been married going on five years with two little ones and another on the way," he announced with pride. Then his eyes focused on Dakota, a shrewd glint visible in their obsidian depths. "Sounds to me like what you need is a good woman, Wilder," he diagnosed before turning away to go about his business.

"No kidding," muttered Dakota. And as he stared into the amber depths of his drink, a picture of a pale oval face with large, dark eyes appeared before him. "Hell and damnation!" he swore, polishing off his drink and getting to his feet. He turned toward the door and halted, narrowing his eyes at the sight that awaited him.

MEN WEREN'T QUITE so frightening after all, thought Sara in wonder as her partner swung her spiritedly around. It had taken her exactly one hour of dancing and laughing and flirting with a variety of partners whose names she couldn't remember to figure that out. She giggled and then yelped as Evan or Tyler or Andy or whatever his name was dipped her at the end of the set. She hugged him as he lifted her up again.

"That was fun! Let's do it again," she suggested, but before she could latch onto him again, she was pulled tight against a larger, harder body.

"My turn, I think," said the cold, deep voice she knew belonged to the warm, muscular chest under her cheek. Curious, she looked up to see who her new partner was. Up, past the white cotton T-shirt stretched tautly over wide shoulders, past the strong, tanned column of throat, past the square, faintly shadowed jaw which seemed to be tightly clenched for some reason, past the bronzed, harshly planed face, and straight into a familiar pair of icy gray eyes.

"Oh!" Her eyes widened. "It's you." Frowning, she asked, "What are you doing here?"

"Dancing."

Sara looked down at the black snakeskin boots, which didn't seem to be moving, then back up into his face. The quick movement made everything tilt crazily for a few seconds and she stumbled before he steadied her.

"No, you're not," she accused. "You're just standing there. C'mon, baby, loosen up and relax. You just keep movin' and let me do all the thinkin'."

She giggled and tried to move away from him slightly so that he could swing her around like all her other partners had done.

Only the rude man yanked her back and tightened his hold.

"Hey, that's not how it's done!"

He was looking down at her with what seemed to be a mixture of suspicion and amusement. "The music has changed."

She stopped trying to twist out of his arms and cocked an ear toward the band. "So it has." She looked down at his feet. "Are those steel-toed boots?"

"What?"

She heaved a huge sigh. Good-looking, but a tad thick in the head. "I'm going to step on your toes, you know. I'm not very good at waltzing."

"We're not going to waltz. We're going to slow dance."

"Oh." She had to think about that one for a minute. "Well, that's okay then."

She relaxed as he wrapped her arms around his neck before placing his hands on her waist. It was surprising how warm and secure she felt in his arms. He started to sway slowly and she took the opportunity to snuggle into his body, tightening her grasp on him and laying her head trustingly against his chest.

"Mmm, this is heavenly," she breathed dreamily as she settled against him.

This was sheer, unadulterated hell, thought Dakota, as he gritted his teeth in frustration. He could feel her soft breasts pressed against his chest, could feel his arousal pressed against her belly, could feel the warmth of her skin through her shirt. Every time he took a breath, he inhaled the fragrance of wildflowers that clung to her hair and skin, and every time she sighed, he felt her warm breath on his chest. And she was so zonked, she didn't have a clue what she was doing to him. He nearly groaned out loud when she started to play with a strand of his hair, her fingers brushing against his collar as she raked them through its length.

He let out a shaky breath and decided to get right to the point. "Sara, what are you doing here?"

"Oh, I'm on a manhunt," she said casually as she shifted against him.

He drew in a sharp breath. Then another as her body brushed against the muscle straining under the zipper of his jeans.

"I see. Why?"

"Why what?"

Hell, she was trying to make him as daft as a duck. "Why are you on a manhunt?"

"Because I need a man. I told her I'd be bringing one, you know," she replied, as if that cryptic statement should have explained all the mysteries of the universe.

"Told who?"

"Mother. But I lied. I don't have a date. I don't want a date. I don't even want to go. But I have to. All their snobby friends will be there."

"Be where?"

"At the party. Their thirtieth anniversary, you know. It's in a month. Big bash. Over two hundred guests. Champagne, caviar, cold and hot buffet, live band, the works. I'm going to hate it."

"So, why don't you just tell her that?"

Her eyes rounded and she laid a cautious hand on his forehead. "No, not feverish. I know, you've been *drinking!*" she accused. "Otherwise you'd remember that Mother doesn't allow herself to be thwarted."

"I've never met your mother."

"Lucky you," she muttered.

He tried to keep his lips from twitching as she gestured him closer with a forefinger, whispering conspiratorially in his ear, "My parents don't like me very much. I was supposed to be a boy, you see. Plus I screw up a lot. But not this time. This time I've found me the perfect man." A coy smile touched her lips and she wagged a finger under his nose. "Kate said you'd be perfect, so I watched you at the barbecue and you were. But then you turned out to be too much fish for my itty bitty pole and I decided to throw you back before you could zip up your pants."

4

WHILE HE WAS trying to unravel this convoluted piece of logic, she continued, "Only now mother's told everyone so I have to keep you." Suddenly, she focused in on his hair and frowned. "Although I don't know how she feels about long hair on a man. Parker's hair is much shorter and she likes him a lot."

"Who is Parker?"

"My fiancé."

He went utterly still. "Your fiancé?"

"*Ex*-fiancé. You're not listening." She yawned. "Can I have another one of those lovely Rhode Island things before we go? Them Rhode Islanders sure make one—*hic*—helluva an iced tea."

"Exactly how many of those lovely drinks have you had?"

She held up three fingers. "Two."

Dakota stared at her in amazement. Jacko's Long Island iced teas were a lethal combination of liquor that could put a hardened rumhound under the table after one swig. God only knew how a greenhorn like her had survived two. Or three. No wonder she was as high as a kite.

"Come on, cowgirl," he ordered, disengaging her arms from around his neck and taking her hand in a firm grasp. "Let's go."

He had to half drag, half carry her from the dance

floor toward the exit. As they passed the bar, Jacko wordlessly handed him a small black purse.

"G'night, Jacko," she yelled as they approached the doors. "I found him!"

"Excellent, luv," he shouted back.

Dakota scowled at Jacko's grinning face as he hauled her out the double doors and set her against a nearby wall.

"Stay put," he commanded. "I'll go get the truck."

But every time he let go, she started to giggle and slide down, as though her legs had turned into a pair of licorice sticks. He tried to prop her up a couple of times before muttering a few choice epithets, lifting her into his arms and carrying her to the pickup. She laughed in delight at this new game, pouting when he set her down against the truck so he could open the door. As soon as she was settled comfortably inside the cab, she started to yawn uncontrollably. Her eyelids began to droop and she was fast asleep before he'd even put the truck in gear.

Dakota glanced at her slumbering form and shook his head in disbelief. What was it about this crazy woman that turned him from a reasonably sane man to a fool on a white charger in a matter of seconds? Such behavior was completely against his nature, yet, for the second time in three days, he had jumped in without being asked and rescued Sara from a potentially dangerous situation.

Of course, his uncharacteristic behavior could be a result of his attraction to her. But hell, he'd been attracted to women before without completely losing his mind. Then again, none of those other women had stirred his body quite like Sara. All she had to do was come within shouting distance and the tightening in his loins would begin. If she smiled at him, he would become as hard as a rock in no time.

He laughed mirthlessly at the irony of it. Just his luck that the one woman he'd responded to in the past six months was the one woman he needed to stay away from.

His instincts told him that she was a *believer*—in love, in marriage, in happily-ever-after—and he'd been avoiding entanglements with women like her for as long as he could remember, preferring straightforward relationships. Relationships based on pure, unadulterated sex. Nothing more, nothing less. The kind where there were no commitments and none were expected. Orange blossoms, church weddings and declarations of love weren't his style. The only thing he had ever been willing to declare for a woman was undying lust and he couldn't even guarantee that anymore.

Sara, on the other hand, was the type of woman who needed commitment, who'd get emotionally attached. He'd learned to avoid emotional attachments at the ripe old age of nine, when his mother had walked out on him and his old man.

He had never forgotten the lesson she had taught him that bright, frigid prairie day. He'd stood quietly in the middle of the hallway while his mother dragged the battered old suitcase through the living room. She stopped to shrug on her overcoat and caught him staring at her.

Dropping down on one knee in front of him, she hugged him. "It won't be forever," she whispered. "I'll be back soon. I promise."

He remembered pressing himself tightly against her, wanting to absorb the lavender scent of her, wanting to believe so badly in that promise.

"Be a good boy and take care of your father," she said, pulling away. He watched silently as she hauled the suitcase out the door and to the waiting taxi.

And then a nameless fear had gripped him and he'd run to the door and yanked it open, screaming for her, but she hadn't even bothered looking back. And that was the last he'd seen of his mother.

He'd cried after she'd gone, great, gulping sobs on the front porch and then he'd wiped his face on his sleeve, blown his nose and begun to close the door on his childish illusions of unconditional love and happily-ever-after.

He knew Sara was different. She still believed in forever; he'd seen enough of the real world to know that nothing lasts forever. A few hours of physical pleasure was all he wanted from a woman, and all he wanted from *this* woman was temporary relief from the frustration that plagued him.

And, at this point, there was about as much chance of that happening as there was of him falling madly in love with the woman snoring gently next to him.

In other words, fat chance.

At that moment, a soft moan sounded beside him as Sara snuggled into his side and tried to burrow her head in the hollow under his arm. He frowned and reluctantly put his arm around her, allowing her to cuddle up against him.

A half hour later, he pulled the truck into the driveway of her cottage and bent over to wake her.

"Sara, we're home. Wake up, honey."

She mumbled something in reply and squirmed to find a more comfortable position on the seat. He sighed and tried gingerly to repossess his arm before climbing out and lifting her from the cab.

"Hold on to me, sweetheart." She slid her arms around his neck obediently. "Are you awake? You'd better not expect to make a habit of this."

She grunted softly, laid her head on his shoulder, and squirmed enthusiastically, wiggling her fanny against a very sensitive portion of his anatomy. "Sara, stop it, will you?" he said, his voice hoarse.

After putting her down on the little wooden bench on her front porch, he dug a set of keys out of her purse, opened the door and carried her inside. He found the bedroom, turned on the light and tried to lay her down on the bed.

Only she refused to let go, tightening her arms around his neck. He tried to pry them off and her eyes finally fluttered open. She stared up at him with those wide, dark eyes and pleaded softly, "Please don't go."

"Come on, you need to sleep this off."

Her grip became almost painful in its desperation. "Promise me you won't go. It feels so good when you hold me. No one's ever held me like this before."

Her confession made something sharp and sweet twist in his belly.

"Okay, I won't go until you're asleep," he promised, tenderly brushing some stray tendrils of hair from her face.

She smiled sleepily at him. "Thank you."

Reaching up, she planted a sloppy kiss on the corner of his mouth before nestling against him and promptly passing out.

NOTHING HELPED.

Not the four headache pills, not the three cups of syrupy black coffee, not the ice pack balanced precariously on top of her throbbing head. In desperation,

Sara had even tried sticking her head in the freezer, but the sadistic little man trying to drill a hole in her head—as if she needed another one—refused to take the hint. It seemed the only way to get rid of the headache was to get rid of the head, and she was seriously considering the possibility.

In despair, she buried her head in her arms and emitted little mewling groans at regular intervals.

"How bad is it?"

Her head snapped up and she let out a bloodcurdling scream when she saw a large figure standing in her kitchen doorway. Then, clutching her head, she winced in pain.

As soon as the pain eased to a dull agony, she opened her eyes slowly, dreading the sight that awaited her. Even without her glasses on, the shadowy outline of an incredibly tall, wide-shouldered body with unruly black hair around a slightly blurred face was enough to confirm her worst suspicions.

Grabbing her glasses from the table, she slid them on. "How did you get in?" she croaked.

He stepped away from the wall he had been leaning against and took a few steps toward her. His face, with its freshly shaven jaw, was harsh in the morning light and his silver eyes stared down at her with an unfathomable glint in their depths.

"Through the front door."

She winced. "Please, not so loud."

He placed a thermos on the table with a decided thump.

She groaned.

His mouth turned up in a grim little smile of satisfaction.

"It wasn't locked?"

"I have the key."

"You have the key. Now why didn't I think of that?" she said sarcastically. Mornings irritated her, hangovers irritated her and he was beginning to irritate her, too. "Who gave you the keys anyway?"

"A little touchy this morning?"

Sara rubbed her fingers against her temples in soothing circular motions. "Just answer the question."

"You did."

"I did." Her head throbbed harder and she began to wonder if an entire construction crew had moved inside. She looked into her empty coffee mug, then longingly over at the fresh pot on the kitchen counter. Perhaps it was time for a humanizing fourth cup. Or maybe another pill. Her gaze fell on the bottle beside the pot. Or both.

"Who else would give me the keys?"

"I don't know," she said absently, getting slowly to her feet and shuffling to the counter. She refilled her mug with coffee and gulped half of it down. "Kate, maybe."

"Why would she give me your keys?"

"I don't know." She was too hungover to think. A stab of pain shot up behind her eyes and she closed them, leaning her head forward until her forehead touched the cool surface of the cupboard. "Forget I said anything. I'm beginning to realize that some things just aren't worth the effort."

And manhunting was one of them. The wretched, annoying creatures just weren't worth the bother.

"What things?"

"Never mind." Picking up the pill bottle, Sara turned it around to read the instructions. "What time is it?"

"Eleven-fifteen."

According to the directions, she still had another forty-five minutes to wait before she could take any more. With a groan, she picked up her coffee mug and made cautiously for the kitchen door. "I'm going back to bed. Please see yourself out."

"You want me to leave?"

"Bingo."

"I'll never understand you, will I?" he asked, sounding singularly unworried at the prospect.

"What's to understand? My head is killing me, I look like hell and I'm not in the mood to entertain you around my kitchen table."

"Funny, last night you begged me to stay and this morning you're throwing me out."

Even hungover, her mind snagged onto the two most important words in his sentence. She stopped and turned to face him, repeating faintly, "Last night?"

One dark brow rose to mock her, but there was nothing amused about the gleam in his eyes. "You don't remember last night?"

Fragments of images bombarded her brain. Soft music. The feel of a rock solid chest under her cheek. Warm, comforting arms wrapped around her. Tender words whispered in her ear. Her cheeks burned. "You mean it wasn't a bad dream?"

He strode to the cupboards and searched them with methodical precision until he found a glass and brought it back to the table. "Exactly what do you remember?"

She watched as he unscrewed the cap on the thermos and poured something into the glass. His movements were controlled and economic, yet oddly menacing.

"Nothing," she lied and, feeling decidedly shaky, sat

down at the table again. "Well, nothing except meeting some giant named Jacko and drinking—" she grimaced "—some iced tea."

"Iced tea?" His fingers clenched the glass as though he were going to crush it with his bare hands. She figured he was wishing it was her neck. He lowered the glass onto the table slowly. "It was a lethal combination of gin, vodka, rum, tequila and triple sec and you were swilling the stuff down like it was tap water. Do you know how many you had?"

She opened her mouth to answer, then snapped it shut.

"I didn't think so. Did it even occur to you to think about how you were going to get home in that state? Did you plan to drive, or were you counting on having some guy take you home?"

Sara remained silent, not bothering to inform him that she couldn't drive and that she never left home without taxi money. Her head was pounding and she was shaking. What had happened last night? She honestly couldn't remember anything except insubstantial snatches past that first drink; all she knew was that she had woken up in her own bed this morning with her jeans and tank top on. The shirt she had worn over the tank had been draped at the foot of her bed. It was obvious now that he had brought her home, but why? And exactly how much had she let slip last night?

"Here, drink this," he commanded in a hard voice, handing her a glass full of brownish liquid. She took it and sipped automatically, then gagged and choked at the first vile taste.

"What is this stuff?"

"It's too bad you didn't think of asking that question last night."

She put the glass down and glared at him.

"I told you to drink it. It's a hangover remedy I used to make for my old man when I was a kid and it tastes like sewer sludge, but that's the price you pay for getting drunk in the first place."

"I've had enough, thank you."

"Drink it or I'll pour it down your throat," he growled.

Throwing him a reproachful glance, she snatched the glass from the table, chugged down the contents and slammed it back onto the table.

After the first wave of violent shudders had racked her body, he wordlessly handed her a glass of water. She gulped it down so fast, she nearly choked, and he had to thump her on the back a couple of times before she was able to gasp out, "Stop!"

She lifted her glasses and tried to wipe her watery eyes with her fingers. "Now that you've finished torturing me, Mr. Wilder, I'd like—"

He took the napkin holder from the middle of the table and held it out to her. "After last night, I think first names are in order, don't you?"

Her hand, clutching a gaily colored serviette, froze in midair and her smile faded. Those two pesky words again. "They are?"

"Ah, yes, I forgot. You don't remember anything, do you?" He smiled blandly at her as he replaced the holder on the table. "That's a real pity considering you had such a good time."

"How...how good?"

"Let's see now. Seemed like you really enjoyed yourself when we danced and—"

"We danced?" She never danced, not if she could

help it, but if she had, it was a wonder he could still walk this morning.

"Uh-huh. And you had an even better time when I carried you out of the bar. Why, you giggled and squirmed your fanny all the way home, if I recall correctly, right up until I got you into bed."

She gulped. "Bed?"

"Now don't tell me you don't remember putting your arms around my neck and kissing me?"

She let out a strangled moan. "I don't think I want to hear the rest."

"Why not?"

She looked at him in disbelief.

"Okay, maybe it was a little embarrassing for you...."

Her disbelief turned to desperation. "Oh, Lord."

He sighed. "Don't look at me like that. Nothing happened, except that you passed out. Call it a funny little quirk of mine, but I prefer my women conscious when I take them to bed."

His women. She was sure there had been many and she was equally positive that not one of them had ever forgotten a moment of their time in bed with Dakota Wilder. He had that dangerous air of raw sexual vitality around him. It was there in his smoky gray eyes when he appraised a woman sometimes, there in the way he smiled that lazy grin of his, there in the overwhelming confidence he exuded. And since she couldn't imagine him being interested in a woman for any other reason except the most basic, another question begged an answer.

"Why are you here?"

Dakota let out a string of silent curses. What could he tell her? That her curvy little body was the only one that had stirred any kind of desire in him in the past six months? That he'd come back this morning because he couldn't seem to stay away? What was it about this woman that held such fascination for him?

There was nothing tangible to which he could point. All he knew was that he'd crossed an ocean to outrun memories of Bill and Foster and the explosion, and he hadn't been even remotely successful until Sara had come along and tangled him up in her life. When he was with her he felt more alive, more excited than he'd felt in all of the past six months combined. But he was damned if he could figure out why. What was it about her that drew him so irresistibly?

He looked up and found his answer in her face, in the direct, inquiring, puzzled stare she leveled at him, in the soft mouth with its hint of vulnerability. It was this hint of vulnerability, this innocence, which attracted him strangely, but these same qualities made him want to turn on his heel and run.

And because he had a highly developed sense of self-preservation, he decided to do exactly that.

Extracting a set of keys from his pocket, he set them down on the table and made for the door. "I came to return your keys."

"Wait!"

He turned to look impatiently back at her. "What?"

"About last night—"

"Forget about it."

"I wanted to thank you for bringing me home."

"And what exactly did you have in mind, honey?" he mocked.

She glared up at him, her big brown eyes accusing. "Why do you always have to be so horribly sarcastic all the time? I was only trying to thank you."

Damn it, he thought, if he didn't know better, he'd swear that the niggling feeling in the back of his mind was his conscience making a return after a very long absence. Lousy timing. "Look, just stay out of bars from now on, okay?"

She shook her head. "I can't. I was supposed to...do something last night and I don't think I got around to it."

"Oh, yes, the manhunt. Wouldn't want Mommy to be disappointed, would we?"

She turned wide eyes to him. "You know?"

"Being plastered has a tendency to loosen one's tongue."

"I'll try to remember that next time."

He replied with an explicit four-letter word. "What the hell is it going to take to make you understand? You can't handle the bar scene. You'll probably end up getting sloshed again and going home with the first lame bozo who throws a line at you."

"I may be a little inexperienced," she conceded, "but I'm not stupid."

"Inexperienced? You're a guppy compared to some of the barracudas out there. Face it, honey, it takes a certain kind of woman to go into a place like Billy Joe's in a hot little red number and come out on top."

"And I don't cut it?"

"If the last few nights are anything to go by, no, you don't."

"You just don't understand," she insisted. "I *have* to do something."

"Why? What's so important about this anniversary party?"

"My mother—"

"Yeah, I know all about your mother. You fed me

that bull last night, but there's something else going on here that you're not telling me."

Her chin rose. "Maybe because it's none of your business."

"I'm making it my business."

"Why are you so interested anyway?"

"Because I've had to rescue you twice now from your little stunts and I don't intend to do it again."

"No one's asking you to."

He ignored her, his eyes narrowing in speculation. "It has something to do with him, doesn't it?"

"Who?"

"Parker. Your fiancé."

She glared at him. "*Ex*-fiancé."

"He's going to be there, isn't he?"

"Wait a minute. It's not what you think—"

"Isn't it?"

"I am not trying to make Parker jealous." She uttered each word through gritted teeth.

He prowled around her small, neat kitchen and yanked his fingers through his hair in frustration. "All right, fine. If you insist on proving that you can get a man, then go to the damn supermarket and pick up a nice, bland accountant."

"I don't want a nice, bland accountant, I want someone like—"

She halted in midsentence and her unspoken words fell like a silent gauntlet between them.

He spun around to stare intently at her. "Like who?" he asked softly.

"Like you."

Her words were clear and precise, as potent and tempting as Eve's apple and equally as dangerous. "Do you know what you're asking, Sara?"

"I'm asking you to help me."

"No."

"You haven't even thought about it."

"I don't need to think about it."

"But—"

"Look, Sara, I'm going back home in two weeks, come hell or high water. I have a business to run and a life I need to get back to, and that party's not for another month. Besides, I don't do the potential son-in-law routine. Believe me, I'm the last man you want to take home to your parents."

"Then help me find someone else."

He laughed, even though the idea wasn't remotely funny. "You're joking, right?"

"No, I'm not. You're a man and you must know what men like."

His first reaction was to refuse unequivocally, but the woman needed to be taught a lesson about propositioning strange men. With grim purpose, he said, "There's a price attached."

She frowned. "You mean you want me to pay you?"

"In a manner of speaking."

"I suppose it's not a bad idea. That way we can look at it as a purely business relationship." Her brow cleared. "How much do you want?"

He folded his arms across his chest and named an outrageous amount.

"Yes, all right. That's fair," she said absently, wondering why *she* hadn't thought of offering to pay him.

Suddenly, she noticed that he'd been silent for the past few moments. She looked up and shivered at the ominous expression on his face. His eyes were suddenly smoldering gray flames in a hard face as he advanced menacingly on her. "You don't get it, do you?

This isn't about money, Sara. It's about us, about this,'' he said, yanking her into his arms and pinning her tightly against him, molding her hips to his so that there was no mistaking the strength of his arousal. "Feel it?"

His hot eyes burned into hers with an intensity that should have been frightening. But it wasn't. She nodded slowly, mesmerized by the fiery gray depths. "It happens every time I'm near you, when I kiss you, when I touch you. It happened when we danced last night and it's happening now, and unless you're willing to do something about it," he thrust his hips forward to make the point abundantly clear, "I can't help you."

Sara stared up at him, a curious mixture of relief, fear and excitement churning in her stomach. Adrenaline pumped through her veins and her heart beat a tattoo in her chest. She saw that wild excitement mirrored in the pulse at his throat, felt it in the hardness of his thighs pressed against her own. Entranced, she touched her fingers to the warm, throbbing spot at the base of his throat and moved them gingerly upward, encountering the faint, blue-black shadow on his jaw, skimming its sandpapery surface, grazing the taut skin stretched over the hardness of his cheekbones, plunging into the dark, silky mane of ebony hair. She had never touched a man this way before, had never known that there were so many textures to discover.

He held himself rigidly, unmoving under her gentle exploration, a muscle twitching at his jaw. She grabbed a rich handful of thick hair and slid her fingers through it, aware that she was playing with fire, but unable to stop herself. He drew her with a powerful, magnetic urgency that exhilarated and excited, making her yearn until she forgot about the consequences, forgot to be afraid, forgot everything except the need that burned within. Her gaze fell on his lips, hard yet oddly sensual, and she ached to feel their warmth pressed against hers once more.

"Kiss me, Dakota," she whispered.

His name had barely left her lips when he let out an agonized groan, and in one lightning quick movement, his lips devoured hers in a hungry kiss. There was nothing tentative about his fevered assault; his tongue sought entry, found it, and invaded the moist, warm sanctuary that awaited him. He thrust and parried expertly, ruthlessly, intent on complete, unconditional surrender. She gave it gladly, her capitulation echoed in low abandoned moans of pleasure. He growled his satisfaction and immediately changed tactics, withdrawing his tongue, only allowing her quick, fleeting nibbles.

Her tongue darted out to lick his lips and she pressed her fevered body closer. "Please..."

The control he had been exercising up until then shattered into raw, explosive need at her entreaty, made him harder and hungrier than he'd ever been in his life.

"Yes," he whispered against her mouth before consuming it, and still he felt as though he weren't getting enough. He wanted more, needed to get closer. Lifting her small body effortlessly, he carried her to the counter and set her down on top, raising the hem of her gown and robe so he could stand between her parted legs, his palms running up and down the silky length of her thighs, stopping to cup her buttocks and press her more firmly against his arousal.

He needed this, so much—needed to taste the hot

sweetness of her lips, to touch the satiny warmth of her skin. The thought of doing just this had tormented him for the past three days, however much he had tried to ignore it. No other woman had driven him so far so quickly, but Sara's touches inflamed him. He slid a hand between their bodies and deftly untied the knot at her waist, parted her robe, and searched for an opening to her gown. His hand roamed her back, then skimmed to the front. She arched and moaned as his fingers grazed her from navel to breast, but he could find no access. Hell and damnation, she was locked up tighter than Fort Knox.

"Sara, honey, where are the buttons on your gown?" he asked, trailing hot, wet little kisses down the curve of her cheek.

"There...aren't...any," she gasped against his lips.

And a good thing, too, said his newly awakened conscience. *Wilder, you jackass, what are you getting yourself into?*

Trouble. Big trouble.

With a supreme effort, he tore his mouth from hers and stepped back, his breath coming in harsh, ragged gasps as he strove for control.

"Dakota?" Her question was a confused whisper.

He looked down at her softly flushed face, at her lips, pink and swollen, and her passion-darkened eyes, and had to clench his fists to stop from pulling her back into his arms.

"I'm sorry," he said roughly. "That was way out of line. Forget I said anything."

Sara caressed his hardened jaw with gentle fingers. "No."

He grabbed her hand. "Sara—"

"Believe it or not, I'm a grown woman and I can make my own decisions."

She felt him go dangerously still. "What are you saying?"

"Isn't it obvious?"

"Spell it out for me."

An electric silence permeated the room as he studied her, his dark gray eyes intense, piercing through her as though they could read her very soul. His concentrated scrutiny unnerved her, broke down her courage, dissolved her determination, and she looked quickly away, knowing that she would need every ounce of courage she possessed to get through the next few minutes.

She gazed again into his dark, intent face and her heart began to pound inside her chest. All she had to do was surrender her body to him. It couldn't be very hard; she'd done it once before. Only afterward, Parker had broken her heart into a million tiny pieces and she still hadn't finished picking them up.

Isn't it about time? whispered a voice in her head. How long could she go on being paralyzed by something that had happened a lifetime ago? She'd sequestered herself from her family, from her friends, from everyone except Kate. She'd lived vicariously through her characters and, for a time, that had been enough. Only it wasn't anymore. She'd already lost two years of her life. She had no intention of losing another minute. From now on, she would be more like Desiree—adventurous, dynamic...a risk taker. Desiree wouldn't run from a challenge. She'd do whatever it took to get what she wanted.

And what she wanted was Dakota Wilder.

"Sara?"

She slid off the counter, pulled together the edges of her robe and faced him squarely, knowing exactly what it was she needed to do in order to pull this off.

"I'll do it," she stated calmly. "On one condition."

5

DAKOTA GRABBED the plastic-wrapped pieces of pizza from last night's dinner, along with an ice-cold can of beer, and kicked the refrigerator door shut.

She was *supposed* to have booted his butt out the front door.

Then he would never have seen her again, his conscience could have gone back to wherever the hell it had come from, and he would have found a monastery somewhere for himself.

That had been the plan. Trust Sara to blow it all to hell and back.

He stuffed the pizza into the microwave, pulled the tab off the can and took a long swig.

Not only had she agreed to the whole outrageous deal, she'd gone so far as to impose her own condition. And all he'd been able to do was stare at her, until she'd looked at him suspiciously and asked, "You're not thinking of changing your mind, are you?"

Hell, no.

He might have had a few inconvenient and extremely uncharacteristic attacks of conscience in the past couple of days, but he wasn't *that* far gone. She was offering him the perfect opportunity to solve his problem. He'd get exactly what he wanted from her with a minimum of emotional fuss. All he had to give up in return were a few pointers on how to find a date.

Best of all, he'd finally get to go home. It had sounded perfect at the time, but the more he thought about it, the more uneasy he became.

It was probably his infernal conscience, this feeling that he was taking advantage of Sara in some way. But their deal was reciprocal. He wasn't the only one getting something out of it; she'd be getting what she wanted, too. Anyway, she'd had every opportunity to refuse. Damn it, he'd *expected* her to refuse! But she hadn't. And, although he wondered at her sanity sometimes, she was right; she was a grown woman, fully capable of making her own decisions. Besides, the condition she had imposed, that she get to decide on the time and place of consummation, gave her complete control of the situation.

The microwave beeped and he took out the pizza, settling himself at the kitchen table. He was halfway through his solitary meal when the phone rang. He got up to answer it, wiping his hands on a paper napkin.

"Wilder speaking."

"Mr. Wilder, I'm putting through a call from Zaire," said a professionally friendly voice. "Go ahead, please."

Dakota checked his watch. It was a little past 2:00 p.m. which meant that it would be after nine at the Macota.

A click sounded over the phone line before Loch's cheerful voice asked, "What's up, Wilder?"

"That's a damn impertinent question, considering the circumstances."

"I see you haven't lost your sense of humor. That's a pretty good sign, considering you've now been in Beaver Creek for exactly...two weeks and three days."

"It's not that bad."

"Yeah, and I'm Saint Peter. Who is she?"

"Who is who?"

"Hey, this is me, Loch, remember? Last week when I called you were begging to come home. I had to threaten you with a month's worth of paperwork to keep you from catching the next plane back. Now you're telling me Beaver Creek isn't that bad?" Loch snorted in disbelief. "What's she like?"

Dakota pictured Sara as he'd seen her this morning, with her old, beat-up, blue bathrobe and scraggly hair, squinting at him through the thick black rims of her glasses.

"Sara's...different."

"Different how? Do you mean she has four heads and a tail?"

"It means she's about as unpredictable as a spitting camel and as stubborn as a Mexican mule, but I'm working on her."

"Working on her? You mean she didn't fall into the horizontal position the minute you flashed that Wildman smile at her?"

Horizontal position? Hell, he'd take her any way he could get her if his conscience didn't get in the way.

"Like I said, Sara's different."

"Better watch it, Wilder. Next thing you know, you'll be registering china patterns and picking out invitations," Loch teased.

"Don't bet your half of the mine on it, pal. I have no intention of getting seriously involved with her."

"Hey, *I've* got the Wildman motto memorized. 'No involvement, no commitment, no hassle,'" he recited. "But, just in case, maybe you'd better get it tattooed on your forehead so *she* don't forget."

"Don't worry, I don't intend to let her forget."

"Too bad. A little involvement might be just what the doctor ordered."

Dakota let that comment slide and changed the subject. "How's everything there? Is Jesse doing okay?"

Jesse Tambo had taken over his position as troubleshooter at the Macota during this extended vacation and, although he trusted Jesse completely, after five years it was hard to just step back and let someone else take over his job. It was one of the reasons he and Loch touched base over the phone at least once a week.

"Jesse's doing great. We had a little trouble with the number two drill on Friday, but he and some of the guys managed to get it going again."

"What about Mgabe? Did you get him to see reason on the production quotas for next year?"

"I've tried talking reasonably, but he's been jerking me around for the last week." Loch's frustration was evident in his voice.

Dakota smiled grimly. Charles Mgabe at his worst was a bureaucratic nightmare, tangling anyone who dared cross his path in governmental red tape, which took lots of time, money and patience to unravel. At his best, he was a worthy adversary. "It's time to start playing hardball, I think. Tell Jesse to fax me the figures tomorrow and I'll start working on a plan. I should be able to take care of it when I get back in a couple of weeks. See if you can't stall him till then. Anything else I should know about?"

He listened intently as Loch outlined all the other minor glitches that had occurred in the past week, interrupting every once in a while with questions and suggestions. As usual, Loch was handling the financial and administrative end of things with his customary efficiency.

Finally, when Dakota could no longer put it off, he forced himself to ask the question that had been eating at him since he'd picked up the phone. He tried to make his voice sound casual, but the tightness in his throat made it impossible.

"Have Salome and Mary made their decisions?"

A moment of static-filled silence hung in the air before Loch answered. "Salome's decided to go back home to her village. She says her family will take care of her and the kids. I've made sure Bill's insurance money gets transferred to her."

"And Mary?"

"Mary likes the job in the office so she'll stay at the compound."

"And the children?"

Loch's curse scalded the phone line. "How long are you going to keep punishing yourself, Dakota? It wasn't your fault. It was an *accident*. Everyone here understands that. There was nothing you could have done. We take all the safety precautions it's humanly possible to take. You know that as well as I do. There was nothing you could have done to stop the explosion."

Dakota leaned his head back against the sofa and squeezed his eyes shut, trying to stem the tide of grisly images that battered his brain every time he thought of the explosion. He and Loch must have had this conversation a hundred times before he'd come to Beaver Creek and, although what Loch said made perfect sense in some detached, intellectual corner of his brain, Dakota couldn't explain to Loch that the knife-twisting sensation in his gut didn't seem to have a whole lot to do with intellect.

Both Bill and Foster had been family men, with

wives who were now widows and children who'd become fatherless in one sickeningly brief moment. He remembered the children, with their dark, shining faces and shy, brilliant smiles, and his hands clenched into fists as the familiar rage engulfed him, followed by a frustrating sense of helplessness.

The images haunted his dreams, devoured his every waking moment, stole every scrap of peace from his life. Worst of all, they whispered questions that echoed ruthlessly, relentlessly in his mind.

Why not me?

Why had he been the one to survive while the others died? He had no family to mourn his passing, no one who depended on him for love and comfort and support. So what was so special about him that he deserved to live while they died?

The questions were like an acid eating away at his soul, but there were never any answers, nothing to soothe him back to the complacent life he'd led before the explosion. There were only facts and he was going to have to learn to live with them. Bill and Foster were dead and there was nothing he could do to bring them back. Nothing.

"Tell me about the children," he repeated.

"You are one stubborn piece of work, Wilder. The children are fine. If you must know, they've been driving everyone around here crazy with those blasted toys you sent last week. You had to pick the loudest ones on the market, didn't you?"

He took a deep, ragged breath as the cold knot in his gut loosened a little. "I guess that means you won't be missing me for the next couple of weeks, huh?"

"Don't even *think* of hauling your antsy ass back

here before then," growled Loch, and hung up the phone.

Dakota returned to cold pizza and warm beer, and helped himself to a piece of the home-baked banana-strawberry pie Mrs. MacNamara had insisted he take home a few days ago.

It had been like that from the first day he'd arrived in Beaver Creek. He'd found the cottage spotlessly clean, all the rooms aired, fresh flowers on the kitchen table, a truckload of food in the fridge and a note of welcome propped up beside the flowers. He'd stuck the flowers on top of the fridge, where they wouldn't be in the way, thrown the note into the garbage without a second glance and holed himself up in the cottage.

But once the food had run out, he'd had to venture into town.

That had been his first mistake.

His second had been going into MacNamara's Grocery and Convenience Store. As soon as he'd walked through the door, he'd become fair game for the entire MacNamara clan. Mrs. MacNamara insisted on giving him books and homemade pies. Loch's cousin Alex insisted on taking him to the Honky Tonk and introducing him around to some of the locals. Alex's wife, Kate, insisted on inviting him—and the rest of the town, it seemed—to family barbecues. Nothing he said or did seemed to convince them that he wanted to be left alone. They just continued to ignore his wishes with the same stubborn, annoying cheerfulness that made him want to strangle Loch sometimes.

Now, not only was he obliged to keep up with the Beaver Creek social whirl, but he was also going to have to play Fairy Godfather to a woman who made Mary Poppins look like Mata Hari. And, to top it all off, he was going to have to keep his paws off her until *she* decided it was time to consummate their deal.

Surely guerrilla warfare would have been easier?

He sighed, picked up the L. A. Michaels novel that Mrs. MacNamara had given him and began to read.

THE DEAFENING BLAST of "Satisfaction" reverberated through the front door of Sara's house. Dakota knocked again and waited. There was still no answer, just the rhythmic vibrations of the floorboards under his feet.

He wondered that she hadn't gone deaf yet, and tried the doorknob. He hadn't expected it to, but it turned easily in his hand. He swore under his breath. The woman had absolutely no sense of self-preservation whatsoever.

Feeling completely unrepentant, he followed the Rolling Stones through the living area to a small room at the back of the house, and stopped at the threshold of what he assumed was Sara's study.

Muted sunlight filtered in through the drawn curtains, casting a soft pink glow through the room. A floor-to-ceiling bookshelf housed the stereo which was doing the dirty deed. A black leather love seat occupied the opposite wall, the space above it adorned by six large, framed posters. His gaze slid from one to the other, noting the identical black backgrounds, the bloodred insignias in the middle, and the titles in bold white: *January in Johannesburg, February in Freeport, March in Madrid, April in Anchorage,* and *May in Macao.* Scrawled across the bottom, also in white, was the name L. A. Michaels.

He frowned for a moment, remembering his conversation with Mrs. MacNamara on the night of the storm.

He walked farther into the room, his attention now riveted on the small figure at the massive desk beneath the window. Her face turned away from him, her hair wound turban-style in a towel, her bare legs wrapped around the chair, Sara seemed completely absorbed in her task. She was staring at the computer screen in rapt concentration, her fingers flying over the keyboard. Pausing for a few seconds, she reached absently for the tall glass sitting on the desk and sipped before resuming her work.

His gaze fell on the exposed curve of her throat, delicately arched, and he experienced a sudden urge to touch his lips to the temptingly bare flesh, to taste the pale, smooth skin, to inhale the sweet fragrance of wildflowers that was always with her.

Instead, he walked to the stereo and flipped it off, plunging the room into sudden silence. She didn't miss a stroke. The rhythmic tapping of her fingers striking the keys punctuated the silence.

Leaning against the shelf, he folded his arms in front of him, watching as she extended one gracefully pointed foot behind the other, touched her toe to a bare calf, and gently slid it up and down. He shook his head. If only Loch could see him now. Aroused simply by the sight of a woman's neck and calves. Incredible.

"Okay, Jon, now that you've managed to escape from the Turkish prison, what do you want to do next?"

"I imagine a shower and a change of clothes would come in handy right about now," he drawled.

She screamed and swung herself around in surprise, her eyes wide with fright, one hand pressed to her chest.

"Oh, jeez, would you stop that!"

"Stop what?"

"Sneaking up on me like that. You scared me half to death!"

"I could have done a lot more than that. Don't you know better than to leave your door unlocked?"

"Nobody around here locks their doors during the day."

"From now on, you can be the exception."

She scowled at him. "What are you doing here so early anyway?"

"Early? Honey, didn't your mother teach you how to tell time?"

She checked her watch and sent him a stricken look that was at odds with the fact that it was only five minutes after their appointed time. "I'm sorry. I didn't mean to do this. Honest. It's just that I had an idea for a scene and I—"

"Relax, Sara. It's okay."

She jumped out of her chair. "It'll only take me a minute to get ready."

"Hell, take five."

"Thanks. I'll just—"

He sighed. "I was kidding."

"Oh. *Oh.*" A sheepish smile tugged at the corners of her lips and she relaxed visibly. "I get a little crazy sometimes when I'm working."

"You mean like talking to your characters and expecting them to talk back?"

"Yes, I..." She trailed off, her expression becoming suddenly guarded. "You know."

"The posters and the comment to Jon did you in."

She turned away and busied herself with the computer.

"Why all the secrecy?"

"I like my privacy. Besides my editor, my agent and Kate, no one knows."

"Except me."

She looked at him again. Her gaze met his and he caught a glimpse of the wary resignation reflected in her eyes. "Except you."

He thought about pressing her and asking if it was the need for privacy that had brought her to Beaver Creek, or if she was running from something else. But he caught himself in time. It was none of his business.

"Don't worry, your secret's safe with me."

She switched off the computer and turned to face him. "Thank you."

He looked down at her, dressed once again in that infernal blue bathrobe. She had a towel wrapped around her head. She stood uncertainly in front of him, her face scrubbed clean, her skin temptingly soft and flushed, her wide chocolate-brown eyes staring at him with what seemed to be a mixture of doubt and apprehension. At that moment he felt it again, that strange combination of gut-deep desire and aching tenderness. The desire he could handle. It was the other that made him uneasy. He'd flirted with women before, charmed them, brought them pleasure in bed, but he'd never felt the urge to wrap one in his arms before, to soothe and gentle her with soft kisses.

He didn't want to feel it now, either.

Deliberately, he shifted his gaze from her face down to her body. "Does inspiration usually strike when you're in the shower?"

Her gaze followed his and she flushed, clutching the rapidly slipping towel with one hand and the neckline of her robe with the other. "I'll go change now. Excuse me."

"Oh, don't bother on my account. I'm beginning to find that robe very sexy. Not to mention convenient," he said, looking pointedly at the loosely knotted belt.

She walked to the door backward, trying to tighten the belt and keep the towel from slipping. "I'll be right back."

Turning, she fled the room.

He thrust his hands into the pockets of his jeans and strolled around the room. He stopped in front of the posters and studied them closely, wondering why he wasn't more surprised at finding out about Sara's secret identity. He supposed that in some strange, cosmic corner of his mind, it all made perfect sense. He'd read both of the books Mrs. MacNamara had recommended. Yesterday, as a matter of fact, since it had been an off day on the MacNamara social calendar. Her books were full of fascinating characters, a continuous stream of action and adventure, complicated webs of intrigue, and an irresistible, quirky sense of humor that was undeniably Sara. He'd enjoyed them so thoroughly, he'd even gone back this morning to buy the rest of the series, much to Mrs. MacNamara's delight. And knowing that Sara had created them just made him all the more curious about what other fascinating secrets lay under that unassuming exterior of hers.

Not that he could afford to indulge his curiosity.

No involvement, no commitment, no hassle.

He reminded himself that the only reason he was here at all was to keep his end of their bargain. The sooner he managed it, the sooner she'd have to keep her end, and the sooner he'd be able to go home. And, as far as he was concerned, sooner was definitely better.

SARA RETURNED to find Dakota standing in front of the bookshelf, leafing through a volume on weaponry. She hesitated on the threshold, running a hand over her braided hair to make sure it was neat. He looked up, his gaze raked her up and down and he quirked a dark brow.

"Adequately fortified?"

"I beg your pardon?"

He replaced the book on the shelf and approached her with slow, deliberate steps until he was standing directly in front of her, staring into her eyes with a mesmerizing intensity.

"I warned you yesterday, Sara. You have something I want very badly and I intend to get it," he caressed her cheek with gentle fingers, "and those big brown eyes and a few dozen pearl buttons aren't going to stop me. Unless you've changed your mind."

She took a shaky step back. "I haven't changed my mind."

"Good." He smiled, a slow, wicked smile that had the same effect on her stomach as a blowtorch on a stick of butter. He slid his hand from her cheek to the top button on her white cardigan. "Then let's get rid of this. It's much too hot out for a sweater."

Sara held her breath and watched in helpless fascination as his long, tanned fingers slipped the first pearl through the buttonhole, then skimmed down to the next one. The knuckles of his right hand grazed her breast in the process and she had to bite her lip, willing herself not to react to his touch.

He continued his task in a leisurely manner, stroking the nubby cotton lightly when he finished. "Did you make this yourself?"

She nodded, surprised that he'd noticed.

"A woman of many talents," he murmured, and slipped the garment off her shoulders, exposing bare flesh and her tank top.

"You don't play fair, do you?" she whispered.

He held out the sweater to her. "Not when I want something as badly as I want you."

A long, slow shiver rippled down her spine.

She hadn't anticipated this. Yesterday, when she had imposed her condition, she'd done it in order to buy herself some time. Despite the fact that she was determined to be more like Desiree, adventurous and spontaneous and free, she knew herself well enough to realize that the transformation wouldn't happen overnight. She would need some time to work herself up to the idea of going to bed with Dakota Wilder. Not physically—what had just happened was proof enough that he could arouse her simply with a look or a touch—but emotionally. She wanted him, but she needed to spend some time with him, to get to know him at least a little before she allowed him to seduce her.

Which meant that the next two weeks were going to be a pitched battle between his desire and her willpower.

Sara stared into his smoky gray eyes, full of sensual promise, and decided that at this moment retreat was the better part of willpower. She seized the sweater from his hands and took a couple of steps backward. Sliding her tongue over dry lips, she forced herself to ask, "What did you want to talk to me about today?"

His answering smile was slow and dangerous. "Guerrilla warfare."

DAKOTA LEANED against the back of the canoe with a satisfied sigh and propped his booted feet on top of the wooden slat in front of him. He was glad Sara had suggested they go out to her garden to talk, but as soon as he'd seen the upside-down canoe on her little dock, he'd convinced her to paddle out to the middle of the small lake. It was surprisingly quiet at this time of the morning, the only audible sounds those of the waves slapping against the sides of the wooden canoe. He closed his eyes, letting the gentle bobbing motion of the boat and the soft breeze soothe him.

"Were you ever in the army?"

He opened one eye and squinted at Sara. She sat cross-legged across from him, the straw hat she wore shielding her face from the burning rays of the sun.

"Yeah, I guess you could call it that."

"Did you ever suffer from a severe head wound?"

"No, why?"

"Because that's the only explanation I can think for such an asinine idea."

He raised a questioning brow at her.

"What the heck does guerrilla warfare have to do with finding a date?"

"Same concept. You and I, a small, independent force, are going to wage a slightly unorthodox war against the army of poor, unsuspecting single men out there."

She cocked her head sideways. "Wouldn't that make you a traitor?"

"No, technically, it makes me a mercenary."

The implication of his statement, that he wasn't helping her out of the goodness of his heart, but because he expected payment for his services, wasn't lost on her. A quick tide of pink invaded her cheeks, but he had to give her credit. She didn't look away.

"The first thing we need to do is devise a strategy."

"A strategy?"

"A plan of attack. We need to choose our target for maximum impact, and based on his weaknesses, we decide which tactics are going to be most effective. Lastly, we engage our forces in a quick, clean strike."

"Our forces?"

"You."

"Me."

"Do you think you could stop repeating everything I say?"

"I'm sorry, it's just that this whole warfare thing sounds so...so..."

"Logical?"

"*Stupid.*"

"Trust me. I know what I'm doing."

"Do I have a choice?"

"You always have a choice. You can trust me, or you can try to find a date by yourself again."

After a small silence, she asked brightly, "So, how do we decide on the target?"

He stifled a smile. "We go on a reconnaissance mission."

"A reconnaissance mission," she repeated, then threw him an apologetic look. "Sorry."

"Basically, it means we go into enemy territory and scout a target. Or, in this case, two or three. We see what their habits and weaknesses are. Then we make up a plan of attack, a step-by-step list of how to accomplish our mission based on what we've observed."

"And you think this...this plan of attack is going to work?"

"Strategic planning is the key to every successful mission."

"Were you really in the army?"

"Several, in fact. Mostly private ones."

She leaned forward and stared at him incredulously as the weight of his statement sank in. "A mercenary? You really *are* a mercenary?"

"Was," he corrected.

Her face lit up, a bright, excited glow coming into her brown eyes. "Just like the Jaguar!"

"The Jaguar?"

"McAllister's nemesis in my latest book. This is so incredible! He looks just like you. I even pictured him wearing black snakeskin cowboy boots. When I first saw you at Billy Joe's that night, I thought I was hallucinating, which sort of explains why I acted like such a blithering idiot when you showed up." She laughed and shook her head.

Her laughter was joyous, uninhibited, and it struck him suddenly that this was the first time she'd allowed him to see her, the real Sara who hid beneath the wary, defensive, shy exterior. And he saw something that he suspected very few people took the time to see.

She was breathtakingly beautiful.

For a moment, he felt a sense of exhilaration, the same sense of exhilaration he felt when months of tough, frustrating negotiations finally culminated in that single, firm handshake that signaled success.

"Would you mind if I picked your brain sometime? I've been using books to do most of my research, but there are a couple of things I haven't been able to find adequate references on. I don't usually get the opportunity to do live research. This is so exciting!"

He grinned at her. "Everything is grist for the mill, huh?"

She nodded, smiling guiltily. "Almost everything. I

can't seem to help it. Feel free to say no if you don't want to talk about it."

"I'm flattered, actually. I suspect not many people get to have an imaginary clone in an L. A. Michaels book."

"You'd be surprised. Remember Jacko, the bartender at The Honky Tonk?"

"Don't tell me. There's a beefy, bald-headed bartender somewhere in McAllister's near future."

"I'm afraid so."

"Why spy thrillers? You don't exactly strike me as the type."

"Why? Because I'm not a man?"

"Because you're so bloody naïve in real life. I can't imagine you sitting there masterminding ways to torture McAllister."

She grinned. "Like I said, you'd be surprised. I did a pretty good job on my mother when I was a kid. I used to drive her nuts. All the other girls wanted dolls and tea sets to play with. I wanted books. I read everything I could get my hands on. When I got older, I discovered Louis L'Amour and Zane Grey and Ian Fleming and Robert Ludlum. I thought I'd died and gone to heaven. The other girls used to have sleepovers and put on makeup and do their hair and talk about boys, but I just wanted to sit by myself and daydream. Do you know what I'd dream about?"

"I'm guessing it didn't have anything to do with June Cleaver," he said dryly.

"I used to dream about James Bond."

"You and every other female old enough to breathe."

"No, I mean I used to dream I *was* James Bond," she explained. "I loved the idea of going after bad guys with nothing more than those weird gadgets Q was always inventing. And all those exotic locations..." She sighed, a far-off look of longing coming into her eyes.

He watched her curiously, wondering why it was that she'd ended up here in Beaver Creek, when her love of travel and adventure was so obvious, in her eyes and, now that he thought about it, in her books.

"Have you traveled a lot?"

She shook her head and he heard the wistfulness in her sigh. "I haven't really been anywhere exotic. I've never had the courage to go by myself."

"So you write about all the places you'd like to see instead?"

"Yes."

"You're very talented."

A tinge of pink touched her cheeks. "Thank you."

"Mrs. MacNamara says most of Beaver Creek thinks you are, too. She peddles your books pretty good."

"I know. It's embarrassing sometimes when I go in there and she's pushing them. Especially when she does it to me. I never know what to say."

"Why not the truth?"

"I guess I'm scared that once people find out who L. A. Michaels really is, they'll point and laugh and stop buying my books. Pretty stupid, huh?"

He thought of his own fears, secreted away in the deep recesses of his soul. Fear that he'd turn out like his old man, so obsessed with one woman that, when she left him, he hadn't cared about anything, not even his young son. Instead, he'd spent the next six years deliberately trying to kill himself with booze. He'd succeeded too, leaving behind a fifteen-year-old kid to face the world alone.

"No, not stupid. Just human, I guess."

Suddenly, she laughed again. "After I saw *Octopussy* I begged my mother to go to India."

"What'd she say?"

"She said I was a very peculiar child and she didn't know why I couldn't be like all the other girls and go to tennis camp instead. So I figured that if I couldn't really go there, I'd pretend. I used to spend hours making up stories."

"What did she think about that?"

"She hated my 'scribbling,' as she called it. She said I was wasting my life daydreaming when I should have been learning how to do important things."

"And her definition of important things was...?"

"Learning how to dance gracefully. Being a witty conversationalist and a gracious hostess. Learning how to play tennis and flirt." She grimaced. "All the things that would help me attract and become a useful wife to an important man. I tried hard to please her, but I was never any good at those things."

"What happened next?"

"College."

"What did you major in?"

"Business administration and accounting."

He looked at her in surprise. He'd fully expected her to say shopping or hostessing.

"Yeah, that was pretty much my reaction, too. I guess she figured if I couldn't be a useful wife, maybe I could be a useful daughter in my father's firm. And, before you ask, the only good thing about college was the creative writing course I took as an elective."

"So, I guess you didn't make it into the big, bad world of business?"

"It took exactly five months, three weeks and one day before my father could convince my mother that if she didn't want to lose everything they'd ever worked for, she should gently steer me in another direction. For the next three years, I played dutiful daughter by day, and she paraded eligible gentlemen past me by night. I scared them all off."

"Deliberately?"

"I only wish I'd been capable of doing it deliberately. It got so that every time a man came near me, I'd turn into a klutz. I stepped on their toes, spilled things on them, you name it. When they tried to talk to me, I'd stutter or turn into a mute. The harder I tried, the worse it got. One day, I was just sitting in my room thinking what it would be like to be anyone I wanted to be and that's when I came up with Jon McAllister. The rest, as they say, is history."

"What about Desiree?"

A small, mischievous smile played on her lips. "After *February in Freeport*, Jon began to get a little too cocky. I figured he needed his comeuppance. Desiree was just the person to give it to him."

"Is she a real person, too?"

Her smile faded slowly and she looked away. "No, she's the antithesis of a real person."

Even though he suspected the answer, he asked. "Who?"

She stared out across the water. "Me. Desiree is everything I'm not. She rides a Harley and plays pool and drinks tequila. She's adventurous and gutsy and spontaneous and a risk taker. She goes after what she wants." She turned to face him, a determined glint in her eyes. "And from now on, that's what I'm going to do, too. No more being a wimp. I'm going after what I want."

"Which is what?"

"I want a date for that party. And if he happens to be the kind of man who's going to knock Parker and my mother and their friends on their snobby butts, even better."

"And after that?"

"What do you mean?"

"After the party? Then what happens? Are you going to come back here and keep living like a hermit?"

She frowned. "Where else would I go? Back to Toronto?"

He shrugged.

"I don't think I could live with my parents again."

"You wouldn't have to. You're a grown woman. You can do anything you want. Get an apartment or a house of your own. Travel."

She lifted her chin in what he was beginning to recognize as a stubborn angle. "I like it here. It's quiet and nobody bothers me. I can write in peace."

And the rest, her tone implied, was none of his damn business.

6

SHE HAD the absolute worst taste in men, ever.

After a couple of hours of reconnoitering, he'd had his suspicions. By the time lunch rolled around, he was completely convinced of it.

It seemed to him that Sara possessed a natural instinct when it came to men, one that allowed her to home in, without fail, on the dregs of the male species. Of the battalion of eligible men they'd scouted in and around the county today, none of the ones she'd picked had been even remotely suitable. While she'd been busy cataloguing their height and eye color and fawning over the cuteness of their assorted children and pets, he'd been watching for other things. And from what he'd seen so far, it was a wonder that the women around here hadn't mass migrated to another planet.

Of course, Sara hadn't seen it that way. It had taken all of his not inconsiderable powers of reasoning, coercion, ingenuity and intimidation to extricate her from the situations she'd managed to get herself into during the past six hours.

And if she asked him *that* question one more time...

"What was wrong with him?"

Dakota clenched his jaw and turned the truck out of the library parking lot.

"I thought he was perfect. He had those gorgeous blue-green eyes and—"

"While you were staring at his eyes, I don't supposed you noticed what he was reading, did you?" he ground out.

"No," she confessed in exasperation.

"Well, next time you meet up with him in the library, ask him what he knows about sado-masochism and ritualistic sex."

"So he was reading a book on it. Big deal. I take out books on poisons and mountain climbing and detonating bombs. That doesn't mean I'm going to go out and jump off a cliff or blow up a car. Besides," she said defensively, "I wasn't planning on having sex with him."

Dakota felt a cold shudder rush through him at her words. Sometimes, Sara terrified him. He wondered what she would do once he was gone. Who would protect her from the hordes of men out there, waiting to pounce on a sexy, talented woman? He knew they were out there and the one thing that scared him the most was that they were probably all just like him.

Coldhearted bastards who weren't above using a woman to get what they wanted.

"Did you really want to take the chance that he was researching a book?"

She sighed. "No."

"Look, honey, you have to stop being so naïve about the type of people that are out there. Not everyone is what they appear to be." He turned toward her, a sudden, inexplicable sense of urgency rushing through him. "Promise me you'll be careful."

"Of course I will. So long as you promise that there will be no more scenes like the one in the library. I've never been so embarrassed in my life!"

He raised a disbelieving brow.

"Okay, so I have, but I'll never be able to face the librarian again after what you did and that's the only decent library in the county."

A tiny niggle of guilt pricked at Dakota's conscience, but he squashed it down. "I only had your best interests at heart."

She snorted inelegantly. "Great, I'll remember that next time Mr. Right comes along and you scare him off!"

"Trust me, Sara, none of those guys was even close."

"Next time, do you think you could just *tell* me that instead of letting all and sundry know that Mother Superior sent you because she was—Let's see, how did you put it?—'anxious for me to return to the nunnery before I became morally corrupted by the outside world?'"

He grinned as he remembered the stunned look on her face when he'd made his grave announcement in the little county library. Like a cross to a vampire, his revelation had neatly killed any interest Mr. Gorgeous Green-Blue Eyes might have had in Sara. In fact, the guy hadn't been able to exit the library fast enough. "It did the job, didn't it?"

"You are diabolical. Why are we turning into the supermarket?"

"Remember that nice, bland accountant we talked about the other day?"

She groaned.

"He's in there somewhere and we're going to find him."

"I'd rather he stayed lost," she muttered.

He slid the truck smoothly into a parking spot and

turned off the ignition. "The trouble with you is that you don't know what's good for you."

Her eyes shot brown sparks at him. "And you do?"

He shrugged. "I've been around longer."

"What you mean is that you're more cynical."

"And you're too damn trusting for your own good," he said impatiently, opening his door. "I mean it, Sara. We've wasted enough time. This time, I'll pick the target and you just concentrate on reeling him in. Got it?"

His only answer was the slamming of the passenger side door.

HE HAD THE WORST taste in men, ever.

She'd suspected as much as the day progressed, but now, as she stood in the canned food aisle between the pineapples and the Spaghettios, spying on the target he'd picked out for her to "reel in," she was convinced of it.

It wasn't the target's looks that put her off, although he did remind her rather eerily of a Russian mole named Karl in *April in Anchorage*: short, skinny, dark hair, receding hairline, largish nose, wire-framed glasses.

No, there were other, more important things to look for, and that's exactly what she'd been doing for the past ten minutes. She'd followed him, furtively, of course, first through the produce section, then through the dairy section, and what she'd discovered had appalled her.

He'd snubbed the sweet little girl who'd smiled at him in front of the apples.

He'd grabbed the last carton of strawberries, practically taking them out of the gnarled hands of the elderly gentleman who'd reached for them first.

He'd eaten a whole bunch of grapes without paying for them first.

And even if he wasn't so horrible, how could she possibly respect a man who stocked up on tofu and Brussels sprouts and skipped the ice cream section without even a second glance?

Wrinkling her nose in distaste, she visually followed Karl the mole from the dairy section to the meat section, and wondered just how she was going to approach him. He disappeared behind a large stack of canned dog food and reappeared in front of the taste test counter, where an attractive young woman was handing out tiny cups of fruit juice. The woman greeted him with a smile and offered him a cup, which he took without hesitation. He drank the juice and held out the cup for another serving.

The woman refilled his cup with a polite smile.

He quaffed the juice, leaned over the counter and said something to the woman.

Her smile disappeared and she shook her head.

Sara frowned. It looked like...but it couldn't possibly be. Surely he wouldn't dare, not in the middle of the supermarket! But when he grabbed the poor woman's hand and leered suggestively at her, Sara knew exactly what he was up to.

Karl the mole was making a pass at the taste-test lady.

And the lady wasn't interested. She was looking around helplessly, obviously unsure of how to get her hand back without offending a customer.

Karl the mole, it seemed, despite being sober, was as big a slime bucket as lover-boy Roy.

Without hesitation, Sara wheeled her shopping cart around and headed straight for the taste-test counter, deliberately picking up speed as she neared it. When she was about five feet away, she gave the cart one last push before letting go, then turned quickly away, pretending to be absorbed in the frozen chicken legs.

Seconds later, she heard a crash as her shopping cart collided with Karl's, a scream as Karl's shopping cart ran headlong into Karl, and another crash as Karl went flying, butt first, into the large stack of canned dog food.

Sara allowed herself a small smile of satisfaction.

Mission accomplished.

"YOU REALLY ARE certifiable, you know," said Dakota mildly as he turned the truck into her driveway.

"He deserved it," she said. "And if you think I'm going to have anything to do with a sleazeball like him, *you're* the one who's out of your mind. You're supposed to be *helping* me, remember?"

Hell, after today's fiasco he was hardly likely to forget.

"My memory isn't the problem here."

"Then what *is* the problem?"

The problem, thought Dakota, was that this damn guerrilla war was taking too long and he was rapidly running out of time. There was less than a week left before he had to go back home, which meant he had less than a week to fulfill his end of their deal. At the rate they were going, they'd be lucky to find a target they could both agree on by doomsday.

He frowned. "The problem is our plan of attack. It's not working."

"No kidding."

"We need to come up with Plan B."

"Plan B?"

"Yeah, a backup plan."

"A backup plan."

"I have something in mind, but I need to make a list first."

"A list," she repeated.

He flashed her a look of exasperation.

"Sorry. So, when will this list be ready?"

"Tomorrow night." He leaned over and opened the door for her. "I'll pick you up at nine."

She nodded, jumped out and was about to close the door when he said with a grin, "You know, you have pretty good aim with shopping carts. Ever tried playing with balls and a cue stick?"

"I CAN'T DO IT! No way." Her exclamation came out in a rushed whisper. "You're not serious, are you?"

"Perfectly."

"But it's so big!" she protested, staring at the huge, ugly beast with a mixture of frightened alarm and silent awe.

"It's the only way."

She shook her head emphatically. "No."

"It's perfectly harmless."

"No."

"All you have to do is get on and ride it."

"No."

Dakota muttered a satisfying obscenity, grabbed her hand and pulled her toward the gleaming monster parked in her driveway. The last, dying rays of the sun reflected off the black-and-silver chrome, lending it an eerie, sinister air. Sara gulped and tried to slink away.

He pulled her back.

"It's the only way we're going to get to The Honky Tonk tonight. Besides, you agreed to do it."

"I know."

When Dakota had called this afternoon and asked her if she wanted to go for a ride on Jacko's Harley, she'd agreed on impulse. It could be her first step toward adventure and freedom. Only she'd never anticipated how big and imposing the thing would be in real life, or just how plain scared she would be. She had never been good at anything having to do with power or speed and she had a feeling that this was not going to be an exception.

"This," he explained slowly, lifting a helmet from the handlebars and plunking it on her head, "is a Harley. There are three rules to remember when you're riding it." He gently tucked her hair inside and adjusted the chin straps. "One, always lean into the corners. Two, hang on. Three, never spit into the wind. Got it?"

She shook her head no, then changed her mind and nodded yes when she saw his eyes begin to narrow.

"Good." He straddled the bike in one smooth, agile motion and glanced back at her. "Hop on behind me."

As she approached the beast with dragging feet and a pounding heart, his gaze dropped to her jacket and he smiled. "I like it," he said over his shoulder. "Where did you get it?"

"Garage sale," she mumbled, placing a cold hand on his leather-clad shoulder and lifting a trembling leg over the seat.

The sale Kate had dragged her to a few weeks ago had offered the jacket for a song and the colorful, fiery dragon embossed on the back had immediately captured her interest. It was perfect for the Jaguar and a great addition to her character closet.

And, at this moment, she could use a little of the Jaguar's courage.

She waited with admirable restraint while he slipped on his own helmet, then pulled on black leather driving gloves, and she wondered hysterically when he was going to finish his *toilette* so that she could die and get it over with.

Finally, he turned his head and flashed her a wicked grin. "Ready?"

She had a good mind to punch him in the nose.

He sighed, reaching back to take her hands and place them around his middle. "Like this," he instructed, and started the engine. The black monster burst to life with a powerful roar, startling her.

"Oh, Lord," she moaned, tightening her grip around his waist and pressing herself against his wide back. As the bike started to move, her entreaties to the Almighty became more fervent and infinitely louder.

Forty-five minutes later, the bike ground to a halt. By that time, Sara felt as if she'd been plastered against Dakota's back for half her life. The sun had disappeared and the air had cooled and the only place she found warmth was where her body made contact with his. Being that close to him made her hot and bothered and did terrible things to her willpower.

For that reason alone, she wanted off this bike, away from the warm intimacy of her body pressed against his. But her toes didn't touch the ground on either side, which made getting off difficult. He cut the engine and she felt the bike tilt to one side as he lowered the kickstand.

"You can open your eyes now," he said, lifting the visor on her helmet.

She snapped them open to find that they were in the

parking lot of The Honky Tonk. "We're here," she said inanely, her voice coming out in a hoarse whisper. She'd squeezed her eyes shut when they'd first started moving and hadn't dared to open them since. Not being able to see the world go by in a blur, not to mention having a death grip on the driver, was the key to a smooth ride, she'd decided.

"Sara, honey, are you all right?"

"No," she croaked. "Are you sure we're still alive?"

"I don't know about you, but I'm only alive because it's obviously impossible to bear hug a man to death." He rubbed his midsection. "Damn, woman, how can someone so puny have such a killing grip?"

She peeled herself away from him. "I am not puny and I was not hugging you. I was hanging on for dear life. If I'd wanted to kill you, I would have done it sooner. God knows, you've given me enough incentive these past two days. And furthermore, I would have picked a less harrowing and infinitely more satisfying method. Preferably something slow and very, very painful," she grumbled, trying unsuccessfully to lift her leg over the seat.

"Do you think you could save your mutterings for some other time and concentrate on getting your butt off this bike?"

She glared at him. "I'm trying, you great, lumbering ox, but your bike won't let me."

He broke into a satisfied grin.

"What are you smirking at?"

"I'm *smiling* because you look like a member of the Hell's Angels tonight."

"Well, I don't feel like one," she said under her breath before finally succeeding in getting to her feet. In fact, she felt more like a bowl of jelly right now than anything else, all trembly and jiggly. She had to clutch the back of the seat for a moment to steady herself. Before she could do so herself, Dakota was in front of her, undoing the straps of the helmet, gently pulling it off and placing it on the seat. He brushed an errant strand of hair from her cheek.

"All right?" he asked softly.

Wordlessly, she leaned forward, pressing her face against the reassuring solidity of his chest, and shook her head no. His arms came immediately around her and she took a deep, shaky breath.

"I was scared," she confessed into the warm leather of his jacket. "Somehow, that's not how I pictured Desiree reacting to her first bike ride."

"The first time can be pretty scary, even for a tough bird like Desiree. You just need to practice some more and pretty soon, you'll be zipping along on that thing like a pro."

She pulled back a little and stared up at him in consternation. "Practice? You mean I'm going to have to do that again?"

"Uh-huh. On the way home."

"Dakota?"

"Yeah, babe?"

"Do you think we can go inside? I could use a nice, stiff drink right about now."

JACKO GRINNED down at Sara. "Don't worry, luv. She's a virgin, more's the pity. Wilder here would have my hide if she wasn't."

Sara shot Dakota a disgusted glance as she took another sip of the tomato juice he'd taken the liberty of ordering for both of them. "Party pooper," she muttered.

"I'm not carrying you out of here tonight."

He grinned at the face she made, then took her hand and led her to an empty table by the dance floor. She sat down at the table and glanced around nervously, taking in the fact that the bar seemed as packed full of people tonight as it had been the last time she'd been here.

Not that she remembered any of them.

"Relax," he advised, taking a handful of beer nuts from the bowl on the table.

"How can I? I feel like everyone's staring at me."

"You can start by loosening your grip on that glass. That's it. Now let's try smiling a little," he said, popping a beer nut into his mouth and chewing slowly.

She tried on a clench-toothed smile. "How's this?"

"A little less wattage," he said, withdrawing a folded piece of paper from the back pocket of his faded denims and handing it to her. "A broken jaw's murder to kiss with."

"If the next target is anything like Karl the mole, I'll pass, thanks," she said, unfolding the lined sheet of paper and scanning its contents. "What's this?"

"Our revised plan of attack. Who's Karl the mole?"

"The lech from this morning. He looked like the Russian mole from *April in Anchorage.*" She frowned. "I don't understand. Where's the part about actually finding a target and reeling him in?"

"The beauty of this plan is that we don't have to. Instead, we're just going to concentrate on giving you the social skills necessary to get you any man you want. That way, you won't need me and even when I'm gone, you can still carry on with your manhunt." Then, at her incredulous look, he added, "Think of it as combat training."

"Combat training," she repeated.

He picked up another handful of nuts. "Trust me. It's a perfect plan."

And it *was*. He'd spent all day working out the logic of it. By focusing on her skills instead of on finding the perfect man, his demented conscience and its sidekick, chivalry, couldn't get in the way of fulfilling his end of their deal. It would no longer be up to him to screen any potential candidates or to worry about protecting Sara. Moreover, it couldn't take more than a few days for her to get through this list. Once she'd mastered all the tasks, he'd be home free.

"It's a ridiculous plan. Look at this," she said, reading from the list. "'Number three. Find out all you can about a potential suitor. Ask questions about his job, family, hobbies and interests, etc.' I can't do that. It's...it's being nosy."

"So, what exactly did you think you were going to do with your target once you picked him out? Hit him over the head with a club and drag him to your cave?"

She glared at him.

"You need to learn how to do this. There's a subtext involved when you ask people questions about themselves. It shows that you're interested in knowing more about them. Or that you're interested, period."

"You mean it's the nineties version of 'What's your sign, babe?'"

"Something like that."

"And look at number five! It's even worse."

"What's so bad about it?"

"'Dance with a man while stone-cold sober,'" she recited and made a face at him. "Stop laughing. I don't dance."

"Take it from someone who remembers last time we

were here. You dance. Hell, you were twirling around out there like Cinderella in warp speed."

"Those were Jacko's Long Island iced teas twirling around on the dance floor, not me."

"You're not going to turn into a coward on me now, are you?"

"I don't have to turn into anything. I've already got a yellow streak a mile wide under this jacket," she muttered.

"Uh-huh. So, you weren't really scared to death of riding on that motorcycle? You were just pulling the old damsel in distress routine for the hell of it, right?"

"If you believe that, just wait until you see the bruises on your ribs tomorrow."

"So you were scared out of your mind, but you got on, risking life and limb, and rode it anyway, huh? Sure you don't want a few more chicken feathers to add to your collection?"

"That was different."

"What was so different about it?"

She threw up her hands in frustration. "I don't know! Maybe because I could scream and hang on to you if I got too scared."

"Well, you've shot my eardrums and my abdomen to hell anyway. What's a few fingers? Come on, Chicken Little." He held out a hand to her. "Let's go dance."

She hesitated for a split second before giving in and curling her hand into his, but before he could pull her up, a deep, cheerful voice interrupted.

"Sara, darlin', is that you?"

Sara looked up in alarm to see a man with a big black Stetson grinning expectantly down at her. He looked faintly familiar, but she couldn't place him.

She nodded slowly.

His grin widened. "We've been wondering when you'd come back."

"We have?"

"Sure, you remember Tyler, Andy and John, don't you?"

"Tyler, Andy and John. Of course," she lied, although the names did sound vaguely familiar.

"Say, honey, how about a whirl on the floor with old Evan?"

Dakota's grip on her fingers tightened. "Sorry, Evan. She's with me tonight."

Sara glanced at him in surprise. His voice had been curt, and the teasing light in his eyes had been replaced by a dangerous glitter that clearly warned Evan to back off.

She didn't understand him. He said he was going to help her, but yesterday he'd done nothing but shoot down every eligible male they'd seen, except, of course, for Karl the mole. Surely there hadn't been something wrong with every single one of them, had there? He ought to be happy that Evan had asked her to dance, but there he was acting as if...as if he was jealous or something. But that was preposterous. What did he have to be jealous about? She'd already agreed to sleep with him and he'd made it clear that he was leaving for Africa in a matter of days. Obviously, he had no intention of having any kind of long-term relationship with her.

So, what was his problem?

"Maybe some other time then?" Evan smiled good-naturedly at her.

"Yes, some other time," she said, smiling absently back at him.

"Well, have a good evening then." Evan tipped a finger to his hat and walked away.

As soon as he was out of earshot, Sara snatched her hand back. "What did you do that for?" she demanded.

"Do what?"

"Chase him away? What's wrong with him? Are his boots the wrong color? Is his head too big? What?"

"Nothing. I just thought that with your dance phobia, you wouldn't want to go out on the dance floor with a stranger."

"Wait a minute. Let me get this straight. You're finally admitting there's a man within a thousand kilometer radius who might be a suitable candidate?"

"I told you, there's nothing wrong with him. I was just trying to do you a favor."

Doing her a favor.

Interfering on her behalf because he didn't think she could handle it.

It takes a certain kind of woman to go into a place like Billy Joe's in a hot little red number and come out on top.

What was *wrong* with her? What had happened to her vow to be more like Desiree? She was supposed to be dangerous, adventurous, a risk taker, not cowering in a corner giving herself fits because a man asked her to dance!

Well, this was it. No more being a wimp. Tonight she was going to be the kind of woman who came out on top.

With grim determination, she got to her feet. "Well, if there's nothing wrong with him, I guess you won't mind if I ask him to dance."

DAKOTA EYED the large hand at the small of Sara's back malevolently, scowling as Evan pulled her closer. Any closer and she was going to suffocate. Damn jackass, didn't he know enough to give a girl room to breathe? And just what had happened to his little coward? She was talking and smiling and laughing up at her partner as though she hadn't been gripping *his* hand like a life-line not five minutes ago.

Damn irritating woman.

Damn her big, soulful brown eyes.

What was the matter with him, letting those eyes talk him into this whole ridiculous fiasco? He should have lured her into his bed, no deals, no conditions. Then he could have gone straight back to Zaire. Instead, he'd been a sucker for a pair of eyes and a smile and look where that had gotten him.

Hard and horny as all get-out and playing Fairy Godfather to a woman who'd raised his conscience from the dead.

He tossed off the last of his drink and looked at the empty glass in disgust.

And drinking tomato juice, for God's sake.

"YOUR BOYFRIEND'S glaring at us."

Sara stopped counting steps and looked up at Evan in bewilderment. "Pardon me?"

"Your boyfriend," he said, nodding over her shoulder.

She turned her head to look and stumbled when she saw the way Dakota was glowering at them. "He's not my boyfriend. We're just...friends."

"If you say so, darlin'. But I'd bet the farm he's none too pleased about you dancing with me. And unless I miss my guess, he'll be coming this way right about now to do something about it."

"I'm sure you're mistaken," she assured him. More likely, he was glaring at her because she hadn't said a word to Evan since they'd started dancing. Being a femme fatale was hard when you were trying not to cripple your dance partner. "So, you own a farm around here?"

He gave her a pleased smile. "My family does, but I'm a city boy now."

"Oh?"

"Yeah, I decided to trade in the tractor for lawyer's robes. I guess you could call me the black sheep of the family. What about you?"

"I, uh, I'm a writer."

"Oh yeah? Sounds interesting. Listen, I'd really like to continue this conversation, but it looks like my time is up."

"You really don't understand. Dakota wanted me to dance with you."

"Did he? Well, then, I reckon he just changed his mind. Smart fella," said Evan, flashing her a teasing grin.

She smiled back at him. He really was a nice man and she liked him a lot. Maybe if she explained her problem to him, he might be willing to help her out—

She was cut off in the middle of her thought when Dakota, his bronzed face set in grim lines, suddenly appeared behind Evan.

"It's a good thing we didn't shake on that bet, huh?" murmured Evan in her ear before releasing her.

Sara stifled a laugh and thanked him before he walked away, but when she looked up into Dakota's dark gray eyes, her laughter faded and all thoughts of Evan disappeared right along with it.

He swept her into his arms without a word, pulling

her hard against him, until every contour of her body pressed tightly against his muscular frame. She had to catch her breath at the wave of erotic heat that flooded her body at his close proximity.

He started to sway slowly to the beat of the music. "I figured I'd better rescue you before he smothered you to death."

"Thanks." Her voice was husky. "Now you can go back to your seat and cross items three and five off the list."

"Put your arms around my neck."

She slid her hands up his shoulders and linked them at the back of his neck.

"Good. Now relax."

Relax? How could she relax when her body was on fire?

"I'm afraid that's not an option right now," she whispered into his chest.

"Okay then, close your eyes."

She squeezed them shut.

"Now feel the rhythm. One, two. One, two..." His throaty voice in her ear, echoed by his hand sliding up and down the small of her back, sent electric currents of desire pulsing through her.

And slowly, ever so slowly, she felt herself succumb to the magic of the moment, felt her resistance melting into the heat of him, until she was floating on a plane of exquisite sensual awareness where nothing existed except the man holding her in his arms. The clean, musky scent of him, the hard strength of his chest brushing against her oversensitive nipples, the soft, silky feel of his hair beneath her questing fingers, and the throbbing heat of his arousal pressed against her belly.

She had no idea how long they stayed locked in their

rhythmic embrace. She only came out of her trance when he leaned down to whisper into her ear, "I don't think I can take much more of this."

"Me, neither," she said shakily.

"Come on," he said, taking her hand and leading her off the dance floor. "Let's get out of here."

7

A STREAK of dangerous exhilaration rushed through Sara as the Harley flew down the dark, deserted highway with a thundering roar.

For the first twenty minutes of the ride home, she felt the same nameless terror that she'd experienced on the way to The Honky Tonk. She squeezed her eyes shut and held on to Dakota's waist with a death grip, her body clenched stiffly behind him. She tried to concentrate on following his movements as he leaned into a corner and straightened, leaned into another corner and straightened.

Then, without conscious thought, she conjured up a mental image of swaying on the dance floor with him. So long as she had concentrated on the soft murmur of his voice, on his body moving against hers, on the rhythm of the music rather than what her feet were doing at any given moment, the steps had come naturally.

She pretended to be on the dance floor now, and slowly, imperceptibly at first, she began to anticipate his moves. Once she learned to focus on the rolling gait of the motorcycle, on the rhythmic sway and tilt of the turns, her body began responding automatically to his until they were moving with a graceful fluidity that was as easy and sensual as a slow dance.

With her fear gone, Sara began noticing other things. Like how warm and solid his back felt pressed against her breasts. How intimately her thighs cradled his hard, firm buttocks. How the powerful muscles in his thigh flexed when he flicked the gear lever.

It seemed that her every nerve ending was keenly attuned to the body in front of her and the throbbing vibrations of the engine against the juncture of her thighs.

The effect was seductive and sensual and arousing.

Exciting. Dangerous. Exhilarating.

A shockingly blatant form of sexual foreplay.

And exactly the type of activity a wild, adventurous woman like Desiree would revel in.

With a shiver of pleasure, Sara closed her eyes and gave herself up to the thrill of danger.

As soon as the motorcycle ground to a halt, Dakota lowered the kickstand and cut the engine, plunging the night into silence.

Thank God it was over.

The last twenty-five minutes had surely been the most torturous of his life and he had the hard-on to prove it.

At first, Sara had held herself stiffer than a corpse in the tundra, but gradually, she'd begun to relax, taking the turns and bumps with the ease of a seasoned pro.

And then, slowly, he'd felt it. The subtle shift in her body language. The provocative, almost deliberate tightening of her arms around his waist. The way her breasts rubbed sinuously against his back with every bump in the road. The erotic way she'd gripped and squeezed his buttocks with her thighs at every turn. It had taken every ounce of willpower he possessed not to pull up on the side of the road and do what he'd been aching to do with her for most of the evening.

Instead, he'd managed to get them to her house as quickly and as safely as possible, and if she didn't get her sweet little butt off his bike soon, he was going to explode.

He waited with gritted teeth for her to untangle her arms from around his waist and slip off the bike. It seemed to take forever, every touch of her hand, every brush of her breast and thigh transforming itself into an agony of endless sensation. Finally, she slid off and he breathed a sigh of profound relief.

Unstraddling the bike, he wondered if he'd ever be able to walk normally again.

He took off his helmet and placed it on the ground, then turned to help Sara with hers. She'd already pulled it off by herself and was in the process of shaking her hair loose. The strands shimmered brilliantly in the lone beam of the Harley's headlight and settled around her face in tousled disarray. Slowly, she ran her fingers through the shiny mass, lifting it from her smooth nape with a grace and sensuality that was innately feminine and incredibly arousing. Then, as if sensing the piercing intensity of his gaze, she looked up. A ripple of heat spiraled in his belly at the expression in her dark eyes.

"Don't," he said, his voice raspy.

"Don't what?"

"Don't look at me like that."

"Like what?" she whispered.

"Like you want to eat me up with this pretty little mouth of yours," he said, brushing a thumb across the soft fullness of her lower lip. "The way I'm feeling right now, I just might let you."

"And how are you feeling right now?"

"Why don't you see for yourself?" he said huskily.

Her gaze drifted down to the zipper of his jeans and she stared at him in seeming fascination. His groin tightened.

Her tongue flicked out to moisten her lips. "What...what if I told you I was feeling exactly the same way?"

"Then I'd say it's time to do something about it."

"Like what?"

"Like this."

He slid his hands across the back of her neck, tangling his fingers in the same dark, silky strands of hair he had ached to touch moments before, and drew her toward him. With her body pressed close against his, he took off her glasses, slipped them in his pocket and slowly lowered his head. Her dark lashes fluttered shut as he touched his lips to hers, sliding his tongue over their warm fullness before coaxing them open and slipping inside. He sampled the sweet, intoxicating taste of her mouth with slow, lazy strokes of his tongue.

She welcomed his leisurely exploration with a soft moan, and he heard the dull thud of her helmet hitting the ground as her arms snaked around his neck in an effort to press closer. Her body melted against his, soft and lush and incredibly, utterly female.

With a groan of raw hunger, he deepened the kiss, filling her mouth with his tongue, plunging deep and thrusting hard.

He'd waited so long for this. A whole day of watching her assess every other man on the planet, of watching her talk and eat and smile and laugh and tease. A whole night of watching her dance with Evan. A whole lifetime of feeling her plastered against him on the bike, touching and rubbing and squeezing him....

All that time he'd waited. And wanted to feel her softly curved body pressed against the length of him, to feel himself buried deep inside her warm, wet sheath, to hear her scream her pleasure when she came.

Now she was in his arms and he was kissing her, devouring her mouth, and she was kissing him back, her fingers clutching his hair in a painful, desperate grip.

Unable to help himself, he slid his hands down her back to firmly cup and knead her buttocks before lifting her and pressing his erection against the juncture of her thighs and grinding his hips in slow, erotic circles.

"Sara, I need to get inside," he whispered hotly against her lips.

A tiny whimper escaped her and she tried to press even closer, trailing soft, hungry kisses across his jaw. Wordlessly, he grasped her thighs, wrapped them around his middle and carried her up the steps to the porch. Bracing her against the door, he unzipped her jacket and brought his mouth to a silk-covered nipple. He flicked his tongue over the erect tip before sucking hungrily on it. She arched against him, her hips undulating against his erection in rhythm with his sucking.

"Yes, baby, feel how hard I am for you," he breathed against the wet circle on her blouse.

"No," she gasped, shaking her head. "Not for me."

"Yes, Sara, just for you. Since the first day at Billy Joe's, it's been like that for me. I don't think I've ever been this hard...." He groaned, taking her mouth again in a ravenous kiss.

She kissed him back hungrily, and when he grazed his tongue down the silky arch of her throat, she tipped her head back with a feathery sigh. "That wasn't me. This isn't me. You want someone else."

He touched his lips to the pulse quivering in the delicate hollow of her collarbone. Her skin was smooth and tender and unbearably sweet under his tongue as he tasted that tiny indicator of her madly beating heart.

"There is no one else, Sara. Just you."

It was true. At night when he couldn't sleep, he dreamed of Sara, of the honeyed sweetness of her smile, the tinkling sound of her laughter, the soft scent of wildflowers in her hair, the unbearable eroticism of her caress, her kiss. He dreamed of touching her, of having her touch him, and he had wanted her for so long, he'd forgotten what it was like to want any other woman.

"Not me," she said, pressing his face into the warm, scented haven of her neck. "Desiree."

Desiree? He didn't want Desiree. She was a fictional character. She didn't exist. He wanted a real, live, flesh-and-blood woman. A woman he could hold and caress and make mad, passionate love to. A woman who could make him laugh and rip his hair out in frustration. A woman who needed a slightly reluctant knight in tarnished armor to keep her from getting into any more crazy scrapes.

He wanted Sara.

Pulling away slightly, he captured her face in both hands, stroking her cheeks with his thumbs. Her skin was soft and damp beneath his fingers, her eyes dark, slumberous pools of desire.

"I want *you*, Sara," he whispered. "Here. Now."

She closed her eyes and for a moment he became afraid, afraid she wouldn't believe him, afraid she'd push him away, and then he felt her entire body shiver in his arms and heard her whisper the one word he'd been waiting an eternity to hear.

"Yes."

It was all the prompting he needed. "Where are your keys?"

"In my back pocket," she said, and leaned forward to lick the hollow of his throat in slow provocation.

He slid his trembling hands from her waist into the back pockets of her jeans, bringing them into even closer contact.

She moaned slightly, her legs tightening convulsively around his hips just as he found the keys.

"Soon, sweetheart. Just hold on a little longer," he urged as he fit the key into the lock.

"I don't know if I can. I've never felt this way before." Her voice was breathless with need as she clung to him and tried frantically to divest him of his jacket. Before long, he was striding through the house, heading unerringly for the bedroom, both his jacket and his T-shirt scattered somewhere between the front door and the bedroom.

He managed to locate the large bed in the middle of the darkened room and eased them down on it. She held out her arms and then he was on top of her, taking her mouth with deep, frenzied kisses that left him hot and breathless with desire. Frantically, he parted her jacket, pulled her top from the waistband of her jeans and slid his hands over her stomach, eager to touch her, eager once again to feel soft, feminine skin pressed against his.

"I want you naked," he whispered against her mouth.

"I want to be naked," she whispered back.

He rolled them both over so she was on top of him, straddling his hips, and before he could help her, she was ridding herself of her jacket and her top, whipping off both with an abandon that was as arousing as it was shocking.

"And I want you to touch me," she said, taking his hands and bringing them to her bare breasts.

There was a frenzied energy in her movements, an urgent desperation in her words that astonished him, excited him, yet made him uneasy. This was a side to Sara he'd never seen before, a side he'd never expected and that was something he needed to think about.

But the sight of her above him, naked in the moonlight, her head thrown back in wild abandon, her mouth parted in pleasure as she guided his hands over her breasts...

He *couldn't* think.

All he could do was feel, feel all the things he hadn't felt in six months, all the things he was afraid he'd never feel again. He concentrated on it, on the sheer, sybaritic pleasure of it, on the feel of Sara's breasts in his hands, on the taste of her nipples in his mouth, on the scent of her desire, warm and musky and sinfully erotic as he undressed her completely.

Then, finally, they were both naked and she was splayed in front of him, her breath coming in harsh gasps, her eyes glittering with a hot, unabashed hunger. In that moment, he knew that she wanted him as much as he wanted her and the knowledge was as arousing as the most potent of aphrodisiacs. Holding her fevered gaze, he slowly parted her thighs and dropped a soft, seductive kiss on the damp curls between her legs.

"Tell me what else you want," he whispered against her.

"I want to be on top."

Her bold declaration sent the heat zinging straight to

his groin. He slid up her lushly curved body, took her mouth with his and quickly flipped them over.

A moment later, she was poised above him, holding his erection in her hands as she guided herself onto him. He watched in fascinated wonder, holding his breath and gasping for air at the same time, fighting to regain his rapidly slipping self-control. The feel of her hands, soft and warm and eager as they held his hard length, seemed a heavenly agony and a hellish delight. Unable to wait any longer, he grasped her waist and urged her down and then he was slipping inside her and she was panting and moaning, grinding herself against him and he was heaving and grunting, thrusting blindly against her. It was fast and hard and deep and wet, just like he wanted it, *needed* it to be. The combination was too good to last and he knew he was finally going to come, now, *now*, and then he did, but it was all right because she was coming, too, and he could feel her shimmering and convulsing around him, and in that moment of triumph he couldn't help but wonder, if this was supposed to be so right, why did it feel so wrong?

DAKOTA TURNED onto his back for what seemed like the thousandth time and scowled at the ceiling. Usually, he had no problem at all falling asleep after sex, but tonight he'd been tossing and turning like a fish caught on a hook. He had a nasty feeling it was that blasted conscience of his crawling out of its hole again. This time, however, he couldn't quite put a finger on his transgression. All he'd done tonight was have fantastic sex with a woman who had seemed more than willing to participate.

Curious, he turned and looked at Sara, asleep next to

him, her body curled into a tight ball, as if trying to protect itself from some dark outside force. He had an insane urge to gather her up and hold tight. Instead, he sighed and folded his arms behind his head.

He didn't understand her. He thought he'd had her pegged as sweet, vulnerable, a little bit shy and a lot inexperienced. Then she'd gone and agreed to that crazy deal of his and ever since, she'd been different.

Sweet, but sexy as hell. Vulnerable, but savvy when it counted. Shy, but flirtatious when she wanted to be. Inexperienced, but oh so responsive when she was in his arms.

But the woman in his arms tonight had been different still. Wild. Wanton. Demanding. It was almost as if he'd made love to another woman altogether.

That wasn't me. This isn't me. You want someone else.

Dakota sat up and swore softly as the truth hit him.

If he wasn't mistaken, he'd just had mind-blowing sex with a woman who didn't exist, except in Sara's imagination.

For a moment, he felt oddly cheated, and then sanity returned. For the first time in six months, he'd been able to satisfy a woman properly. Hell, he should be happy, jumping up and down for joy, not sitting here obsessing because his partner had been more aggressive than he'd anticipated.

Only this wasn't just any partner. This was Sara.

He thought of everything he knew about her, of all the things she'd told him about her life before Beaver Creek, about her fierce determination to find the perfect date for her parents' party. So fierce that she had agreed to have sex with a stranger in order to get him to help her....

He closed his eyes, his gut tightening in dread. If

only he hadn't been so consumed with his own needs, his own desires, maybe he would have seen it sooner, maybe he would have stopped her from doing something he knew she was going to regret as soon as she woke up.

Maybe.

He rubbed his hands tiredly over his face. If he were perfectly honest with himself, he didn't know what he would have done. If he'd realized sooner, maybe he would have stopped; on the other hand, he had no illusions about his character, so maybe he would have allowed his desperation for Sara to go unchecked, regardless of the consequences to her or himself.

Either way, there was no sense harping on events that had already taken place. All he could do was contain the damage and ensure that he didn't make the same tactical error again. Otherwise, his conscience was sure to stage a long and bloody coup, and he wasn't sure if his sanity would survive the uprising.

What he needed to do now was muster some self-control, and then he needed to make things right with Sara.

Soundlessly, he slipped out of bed, found his scattered clothes and dressed, then pulled the sheet over her nakedness, brought her favorite blue robe from the bathroom and placed it on the chair by the bed, along with her glasses.

Gently, so as not to startle her, he touched her bare shoulder. She moaned and snuggled deeper under the covers.

"Sara, wake up."

"Go 'way," she muttered.

"We need to talk."

She groaned. "Need to sleep."

"We have to talk about what happened here tonight."

He waited for the words to sink in, and knew the exact moment she snapped out of her slumber. Her body tensed under the covers and there was a moment of absolute, dead silence in the room. He imagined that he could feel the waves of mortification emanating from her.

"Look, I'll go wait in the living room while you get dressed. Then we'll talk, okay?"

He saw her head bob up and down under the covers, sighed inwardly and left the room.

Ten minutes later, when he'd resorted to pacing out on the porch, she finally emerged from the house. As soon as he saw her, he knew he was going to have his work cut out for him. The old Sara was back with a vengeance, in her uniform baggy sweats, scraped back hair and black-rimmed glasses. She stood by the door, studying the wooden planks with a concentrated fascination.

"Come here," he ordered softly.

Slowly, reluctantly, she moved to stand in front of him.

"Look at me."

She raised her eyes to him, and the expression in them made him wince.

"There's nothing for you to be embarrassed about."

"I can't help it," she whispered. "When I think about... I don't know what came over me."

"Sure you do. You were pretending to be Desiree." He managed to keep his voice matter-of-fact, even though that was the last thing he felt like being.

She bit her lip and looked away. "Yes."

"Why?"

She looked up at him in surprise. "Because that was

the deal. She was what you wanted, wasn't she? She's what all men want."

"And what's that?"

"I told you, she's sexy and dangerous and passionate and adventurous."

"What makes you think that's what all men want?"

"Isn't it? The woman you wanted at Billy Joe's, the one in the red dress, that wasn't me. That was Desiree. It was her dress. And the woman on the motorcycle before. That was her, too."

At that moment, he didn't know whether he wanted to throttle her or haul her back to bed, damn the consequences. He did neither, forcing himself instead to return to the one question he needed answered.

He wasn't finished pushing yet.

"Tell me about Parker. I want to know exactly what that bastard did to you."

SARA TURNED ABRUPTLY away from Dakota's cold voice and walked toward the porch railing. Wrapping her arms around herself, she stared out into the darkness. The buzzing of the crickets in the copse of trees surrounding the cottage seemed to magnify in the silence.

She knew what he was asking and she supposed that, after tonight, he deserved an explanation. Closing her eyes briefly, she said, "He raised my hopes. Made me believe that he wanted me."

"And why wouldn't he?"

She laughed bitterly. "You know what they say. If it sounds too good to be true, it probably is. That was pretty much the case with Parker and me. Remember I told you my mother paraded every available bachelor of her acquaintance in front of me?"

"I remember."

"Well, Parker was the one man she never bothered with. I guess she figured he was a little too good for me. He was handsome and charming and brilliant and sophisticated. He'd worked his way up through my father's company, and he'd never even seemed remotely interested in me. Then, just about when Mother had given up hope that I'd ever attract a husband, it happened. Parker asked me out. One thing led to another and three months later, we were engaged. My parents were ecstatic. Mother was busy planning the wedding of the century, Daddy was making arrangements to give Parker a vice presidency in the company."

She leaned against the wooden railing and slowly ran her hands over its weather-beaten finish, feeling for bumps and grooves in the grain. "For the first time in my life, I felt like I'd done something right, something to make my parents happy. And you know what the best part was? The best part was that I'd finally met a man who loved me enough to accept who I was, unconditionally. Parker didn't want to change me and I loved him for that. About a week before the wedding, I went to his apartment—" She stopped, clutching the railing in a death grip as the memory of that fateful evening returned as it always did, with a startling vividness.

Reality faded slowly, silently. The night song of the crickets disappeared, replaced by the muted strains of Tchaikovsky's *Swan Lake*. The shadowed darkness of the porch was illuminated by gently flickering candlelight, and the cool, fresh night air burned with the sickly sweet fragrance of oriental incense.

She was back in Parker's bedroom, nervous and giddy and excited because, any minute now, he was going to walk through that door. She touched the match to the last candle just as the doorknob turned. She froze, feeling a moment's apprehension that she wouldn't be able to go through with it, but then she thought of the past few months with Parker, of how much she loved him and how dramatically he'd changed her life. Quickly, she scooted into the bed, concealing under satin sheets the white silk-and-lace nightgown she'd bought especially for the occasion.

He entered the room, carrying a bottle and two glasses. In the rich glow of the candlelight, he appeared almost angelic, his blond good looks and tall, lean body a magnet of attraction for the opposite sex. She thought, not for the first time, how lucky she was that he'd chosen *her* to be his wife when he could have had his pick of any woman.

He stopped short when he saw her, a look of stunned disbelief crossing his classically handsome features. "Sara?"

She smiled shyly at him and dropped her gaze to his hands.

"You brought champagne," she said, her voice coming out huskier than usual. "How did you know I was planning to surprise you tonight?"

He didn't answer, just kept staring at her with a strangely disconcerted look on his face.

"It doesn't matter. I have another surprise for you." Slowly, she slipped off the covers and stood uncertainly by the bed, her hands clasped tightly together in front of her, waiting for him to say something. Anything.

"Sara, what's going on here?"

"I know you wanted to do the honorable thing and wait until our wedding night, but, well, I just thought that since we're already engaged..." She took a deep breath and mustered her courage. "I want you to make love to me, Parker. Now. Tonight."

Parker walked to the side of the bed where she stood and leaned past her to place the bottle and glasses on the night table. "Sara, you can't stay here tonight. Your parents—"

"They don't expect me back for a few hours." She slipped her hands around his waist and hugged him tightly. "Please don't send me away. Not tonight."

When she saw that he was about to protest again, she kissed him. Minutes later, he was pushing her back onto the bed and yanking off his clothes with quick, jerky movements.

Making love with Parker wasn't anything like she'd imagined; instead, it had been awkward and painful. When she'd protested, he'd persisted, explaining that it was because she was a virgin and inexperienced.

"It'll be better next time, darling," he said, rolling off the bed and heading for the bathroom. "I'm going to take a shower. Get dressed and I'll take you home."

She lay on the bed for a few minutes, staring at the ceiling and trying to tell herself that at least now she'd be able to enjoy their wedding night. Finally, she sat up and was about to reach for her nightgown when the bedroom door opened. Startled, she pulled the covers back up to her chin and watched in amazement as a woman walked into the room.

She was beautiful, a tall, slim redhead wearing black leather pants and bright red lipstick. The woman paused when she saw Sara, an amused smile playing around her lips.

"You must be the wife-to-be." She walked farther into the room, raising a brow when she glimpsed the discarded nightgown on the floor by the bed. "He didn't tell me you were going to be here tonight. I guess I'm early."

"Who are you?" whispered Sara.

The woman sauntered to the closet, selected a silky dressing gown and proceeded to whip off her sweater, exposing a red bra that barely covered her. "I don't suppose he told you about me, did he? I guess if you're the wife-to-be, then I'm the mistress-to-be, although I'm not too crazy about the term. The way I figure it, you'll always be the other woman because I was here first. Makes sense, huh? Besides, P.J. promised we'd move to a bigger place and travel like we've always planned. Whenever he gets tired of the sweet, adoring little wife and kiddies at home, he'll be coming to me for some excitement." She stepped out of her pants and pushed her arms into the dressing gown. "A civilized arrangement, don't you think?"

A sick feeling churned in the pit of Sara's stomach.

The woman walked to the side of the bed and picked up the satin nightgown. "This is cute, but too conservative. P.J. likes things that are a little more...risqué, know what I mean?"

Sara watched, transfixed, as the woman tossed the nightgown on the bed and turned to the dressing table. She reached for a hairbrush and began running it through her vibrant hair. "You know, I pictured you differently. Not quite so...innocent looking. That isn't the type he usually goes for." She shrugged. "Oh well, I guess it doesn't matter, so long as your daddy still owns the company." A frown creased her brow. "Are you all right, sweetie? You look a little pale."

With a muffled cry, Sara snatched up the sheet and her clothes and dashed out of the bedroom. She dressed haphazardly in the living room, threw on her coat and raced out of the apartment. She heard raised voices behind her, then the door opened and Parker ran out after her, a towel draped around his hips.

"Sara! Sara, come back here and let's talk about this like adults. It's all a misunderstanding. She means nothing to me, I swear!"

She kept running, down the stairs where the doorman stared at her tear-streaked face, wild eyes and disheveled appearance, and managed to get her a cab.

She couldn't remember how long it took her to get home or how long she scrubbed herself in the scalding shower. All she knew was that she needed to escape, from that woman, from Parker, from her parents, from the questions and the recriminations and the lies. But most of all from the utter sense of failure that engulfed her.

"I packed a small suitcase, left a note for my parents that the wedding was off and took the first bus out of town. For the whole bus ride I thought about what that woman had said and for the first time in months everything finally made sense. His sudden interest in me, his reluctance to show me his apartment, his seemingly unconditional acceptance of me. He didn't resist changing me because he loved me, but because he didn't care enough to bother. He didn't really want me—she was the one he wanted. I was just a boring little inconvenience he had to put up with in order to consolidate his position in my father's firm."

"What did your parents have to say?"

"I was too embarrassed to tell them the truth. My mother was humiliated at having to cancel the wedding, and my father was furious that I'd jilted his newest vice president." She turned around, grateful for the darkness that hid her tears, and tried to smile at Dakota. "But all's well that ends well. Parker's an excellent VP and my mother's busy planning his wedding to a nice, biddable young woman named Anne."

"Sara—"

"It's all right, you don't have to say anything. I was an idiot to believe he loved me, but at least I learned something from the fiasco." She lifted her chin and stared defiantly at him. "Men don't want me for who I am as an individual. If I can't learn to take over the family business, or give them an in with my father, or secure their future in his company, then I might as well be wallpaper."

"That's ridiculous."

"I have my entire life's experience to back that claim, so don't tell me about ridiculous," she said fiercely.

"Your entire life's experience has been based on meeting the wrong men. And even if you're right, where does that leave me?" he challenged. "What ulterior motive do I have for being interested in you?"

She sighed. "But you're *not* interested in me. Tonight, it was Desiree you wanted."

"No." His denial was flat, as absolute as the truth in his head. "I wanted *you*. Desiree might be a small part of you because you created her, but she's a fictional character. You're real."

"Parker once told me—"

He turned away from her. "Parker is a jackass."

A few moments passed and she saw him run his hand through his hair before he turned back to her. "Do you trust me?"

She nodded without hesitation, a stray lock of hair falling across her face. Gently, he tucked it behind her ear. "Good, then you know that I have no reason to lie to you. First of all, I'm not like Parker. I don't give a damn about your father or his company. Second, I know exactly who you are and I still want you."

She looked up at him, startled.

He cupped her face in his hand. "There are little parts of you that are just like Desiree, moments when you're brave and bold and sexy, like tonight. But there are larger parts of you that are nothing like Desiree— the shy, uncertain part, the funny part, the demented part that makes me want to bang my head against a wall."

She bit her lip. "I don't mean to make you crazy."

He smiled. "I know. But you do and I like it because it's a part of you, the *whole* you. A woman who is strong and dynamic and beautiful." Caressing her cheek with his thumb, he concluded softly, "And so very, very desirable."

She leaned her face into his hand, his palm warm and reassuring against her cheek. "You're very good for my ego."

"And you're very bad for my libido," he whispered, pressing a tender kiss on her lips. "Good night."

"You're leaving?"

"Yeah. And just in case you decide to get the wrong idea, remember that I still want you like hell on fire, and next time, I intend to have you. All of you. That's a promise."

With that, he strode to the motorcycle, strapped on his helmet, and waited patiently until she was inside the house before roaring off into the night.

KATE THRUST the extra pillows from her linen closet into Sara's arms and headed for the stairs. "So, what are you waiting for?"

"I'm not waiting for anything," said Sara stoutly, following Kate downstairs. "Whatever you're thinking, it's not going to happen. I refuse to embark on a week-long affair based purely on sexual gratification."

"I hate to be the one to tell you this, honey, but I think you already have."

Sara shook her head adamantly. "No, I haven't. That was a one-time thing, strictly business. I kept my end of the deal, now he'll have to keep his and then we'll never see each other again. End of story. Now, change the subject."

Kate let out a long-suffering sigh. "Okay, how's the combat training going?"

Sara frowned. "I don't know. We're about three-quarters of the way through that stupid list and I feel like I'm enrolled in a crash course on How to Get a Man in Seven Days or Your Money Back."

"It's going to be a little hard to get back what you're paying," said Kate dryly, making her way to the kitchen.

Sara watched Kate grab a bowl of popcorn from the counter and head for the freezer. She shifted the pillows in her arms and took a deep breath and confessed quietly, "I'm going to miss him when he's gone, Kate."

Kate halted halfway through opening the freezer and turned around to face Sara, a dismayed look on her face. "Oh, honey, you're not..."

"Don't worry, I'm not falling in love with him or anything. It's just that...I like him. I like being with him. He makes me feel good, you know?"

Grinning, Kate reached for the ice cream. "Yeah, I know. Sounds to me like maybe you should try using some of those combat tactics to get him to stay."

"Don't be silly. He's been up front with me from the beginning, remember? He said he had to go back in two weeks and the time is almost up. Besides—" she followed Kate into the living room "—I can't expect him to put his life and career on hold for me."

Kate put the popcorn and the ice cream on the coffee table and flopped down on the sofa. "Why not?"

"Because he doesn't owe me anything. Anyway, he has this incredible life in Africa. Why would he want to stay here?"

Kate shrugged and grabbed a handful of popcorn. "Because you're here."

"I don't think he'd consider that a very compelling reason."

"Okay, then maybe he should consider staying for the incredible sex."

"Kate!" Sara threw a pillow at her.

Laughing, Kate caught it and propped it behind her. "And speaking of incredible sex..."

Sara rolled her eyes. "Does Alex know you have a one-track mind?"

Kate grinned. "Why do you think he married me?"

Sara was about to throw the second pillow when the phone rang. Kate reached over to answer it.

"Hello?... Yes, she is. Just a minute."

She held out the phone to Sara with an I-told-you-so grin. "It's for you."

8

HE'D TURNED her into a raving lunatic.

It was the only explanation Sara could think of for sitting on Kate's porch at midnight, waiting for Dakota to pick her up.

When Kate had handed her the phone, he'd been the last person she'd expected to hear on the other end. With his usual charming subtlety, he'd ordered her to be ready in two hours.

"Tonight? But I'm spending the night with Kate!" she'd protested, before glancing up to find Kate gesturing furiously for her to say yes. "Yes, all right, I can be ready."

She hadn't even had a chance to ask him where he was taking her before he'd hung up. After last night, though, the scenarios that had flashed through her overactive mind could have formed a video; an erotic, surrealistic one that left her with the strangest craving for a cold shower.

No wonder she was coming unhinged.

She smiled happily into the soft, warm summer night. It was a few minutes before she heard the sound of a vehicle racing down the road, followed by the glare of headlights. The pickup pulled into the drive and Dakota climbed out.

"Ready?"

She stood and dusted off her jeans before walking to

the truck. "I ought to have my head examined for agreeing to this lunatic idea of yours."

"I don't recall giving you a choice."

"Yeah, and that's another thing," she muttered, climbing in as he held the door open for her.

The drive down the dark, winding country roads was accomplished in silence. It wasn't long before he drew the truck to a stop. She looked around curiously, but wasn't able to make out much from the meager illumination of the headlights. It seemed as though they were in a clearing in the middle of nowhere. She turned to ask him, but he had already climbed out and was walking around to her side to hold the door open and help her out.

"What are we doing here?"

"Trust me," he replied.

"Yeah, just as far as I can spit," she said, letting him help her down. He reached in after her and picked up a blanket from the seat before walking to the back and spreading it on the truck bed. He picked her up by the waist, sat her down on the back of the pickup and climbed in after her.

"Now what?" she asked, curious about what he had in mind.

In response, he stretched out on the blanket, folded his hands under his head and sighed in satisfaction. "Lie down here—" he patted the empty spot beside him on the blanket "—and you'll see."

She made herself comfortable on the blanket beside him, closed her eyes and waited.

A few minutes passed in complete silence, except for the buzzing of the crickets in the field around them.

"Dakota?"

"Hmm?"

"What are we doing?"

"Open your eyes and take a look. What do you see?"

"It's too dark out here to see anything."

"Look up at the sky, Sara. See how black it is? Like velvet. And how clear? It's a perfect night for stargazing," he murmured.

Stargazing? She stared at him in openmouthed astonishment, just barely able to make out his chiseled profile in the inky blackness that surrounded them, then turned her attention back to the sky. She blinked.

There were millions of them, a veritable treasure trove of glittering, sparkling gems studding the night sky like brilliantly cut diamonds.

She was unaware that she'd spoken aloud until he echoed softly, "Like diamonds."

"They're beautiful," she breathed.

"What do you see?" he asked again.

"Well, that one shaped like a pot with a handle is the Big Dipper." She pointed it out to him. "And I believe that's the North Star over there. And that's about all I can remember from Astronomy 101. What do you see?"

One by one, he pointed out the constellations to her. Leo the lion, Hercules, Pegasus, the Corona Borealis, and the celestial river of the Milky Way. He had a storyteller's instinctive gift of timing and drama, and she listened, enraptured as he recounted the ancient legends behind each one, the deep, rich timbre of his voice mesmerizing in the soft stillness of the night.

And as she lay there, she became helplessly aware of how much of an enigma he was to her. She'd asked him, a stranger, to help her and he'd agreed. He had held her hand in his and helped her through her fear last night, had captured her lips in his own and tempted her beyond words, had held her body in his arms and given her a pleasure she'd never known before. And it seemed sometimes that he had only to look at her with those piercing gray eyes to know all the secrets of her soul, but she knew so little of him in return, of his life in Africa and why he was here.

She turned to him on impulse. "What are you thinking about?"

Dakota stared silently at the sky. The truth was he'd been thinking about what the hell he was doing in the middle of this field with Sara. He'd been at a stag party with Alex, surrounded by the raucous laughter and noise of fifteen grown men watching a half-naked woman pop out of a cake. And he'd felt that odd restlessness seize him again. On impulse, he'd picked up the phone and called Kate's house, for some reason compelled to hear Sara's voice on the other end. He'd always been a loner, had never needed anyone, but tonight he needed to be with Sara because she made him feel more alive than he'd felt in months. She made the restlessness—the loneliness—go away.

"I was thinking about a telescope," he answered finally.

"A telescope?"

"Yeah, my old man gave it to me on my twelfth birthday."

Looking back, it had been the only worthwhile thing his father had ever given him, that telescope. He'd stared through it every night for hours on end, watching the stars and wondering what else was out there that he couldn't see.

"Do you still have it?"

"We had to pawn it when he got sick."

They'd given him forty dollars for it. Two more days worth of booze for the old man.

"Didn't you get it back when he recovered?"

"He didn't recover. He died when I was fifteen."

"But your mother—"

"She left us when I was nine."

"I'm sorry," she said softly.

He clamped his jaws together, steeling himself against her sympathy. "Don't be. *She* wasn't."

"What happened to you after your father died?"

"Foster homes. There was a different place every couple of months. For a year anyway, until I decided I'd had enough."

"You ran away?"

He smiled into the darkness. She sounded so incredulous, as if running away from home at sixteen was as unimaginable as reaching out and plucking a star out of the sky.

"I decided to go see the world. I was a pretty cocky kid, I guess. I'd try my hand at anything once, so I worked my way around for a few years doing odd jobs."

"You were alone?"

He shrugged. "I didn't really care. Like I said, I was pretty cocky. Life was all one big adventure to me. There were things you had to watch out for, but you learn to take care of yourself after a while. I saw the world and ended up in Africa."

"Is that where you met Loch?"

"Yeah. We'd both hooked up with a band of rebel guerrillas. Had some notion that democracy was worth fighting for. A few weeks, a few adventures, a quick win and we figured we'd be ready to move on."

"What really happened?"

"We got our butts kicked," he stated flatly. "It took over a year, but we were pretty much hooked by then. And there was always another war waiting to be fought somewhere. We had nothing better to do than prove that we could help win it."

"And did you?"

"For a few years, until we finally figured out that ideals didn't have a whole hell of a lot to do with war."

"Is that when you decided to get out?"

He laughed shortly. "No, it took a little more than that to convince us."

"Like what?"

"We were captured by the enemy and imprisoned for three months. After we escaped, we'd pretty much learned our lesson. By that time, we had enough money between us to buy the diamond mine."

She said nothing for a few minutes, but he felt her fingers creep into his hand and squeeze, offering silent comfort. He looked at the small figure beside him in surprise. He'd never had anyone actually try to comfort him before, had never known anyone who'd cared enough to bother. He and Loch joked about their adventures sometimes, but they'd always avoided talking seriously. Loch wasn't inclined to seriousness, and as for himself, he wasn't inclined to talk, period. But he found himself telling Sara things he'd never told anyone else. Maybe because no one else had ever troubled themselves to ask.

He waited patiently for the next spate of questions.

"What's it like?"

He smiled. "What's what like?"

"Africa."

He sighed, wondering how to describe a land of such enormous contrast. He saw it as clearly as if he was there and began describing the visions in his head. The vast yellow of the desert, the rich greens of the forest and the deep blue of the rivers. The scorching heat and the torrential rains. The cosmopolitan cities and the tiny villages. The people he'd met and the places he'd seen. His home and the mine. The sky.

"It's this vast blackness like nothing you've ever seen before. Like the entire universe is spread out in front of you. All the stars, these and others you can only see from the southern hemisphere, all there in the sky above you."

"Sounds heavenly." Her voice was dreamy, far away, as though she'd been beside him, visiting the places in his mind. He wondered what she'd say if he asked her to come back with him to see for herself the strange, wild beauty of a continent that seemed to call to some deep, hidden part of his soul.

She'd probably hate it. The heat, the rain, the mud, the bugs, the isolation, the lack of amenities...the novelty would wear thin pretty quickly for a woman who had been brought up in the lap of luxury.

She shifted beside him and the faint fragrance of wildflowers drifted through the air. He closed his eyes and savored the scent. A few minutes later, he heard her whisper his name.

"Dakota?"

"Yeah?"

"Why did you come to Beaver Creek?"

He opened his eyes and stared at the sky. "The truth?"

"Yes, please."

"Six months ago, there was an explosion at the mine," he said, trying to keep his voice even. "Two of our men were killed and a couple of us were injured. I spent some time in the hospital and when I came out—" his smile was self-derisive as he remembered that disastrous night with Ginger "—well, let's just say I wasn't myself. Loch decided I needed a vacation."

"I'm so sorry," she whispered. "I shouldn't have brought it up."

She sounded so distressed, he found himself needing to reassure her. "It's all right, love."

He felt the soft, warm touch of her hand on his face. "You're okay now, aren't you?"

"I'm fine, but Bill and Foster..." He took a deep, ragged breath. "They were good men, Sara. They had families, wives and kids who need them. It wouldn't have mattered if it had been me, but—"

"Don't say that." Her voice was fierce. "It would have mattered to me. And to Loch and all your friends back home."

"I was the one responsible for making sure everything was safe."

"You're not God, Dakota. You can't control everything. Accidents happen. They were your friends and you would never have put them in danger deliberately."

"If it wasn't my fault, why does it hurt so damn much?"

"Because as much as you'd probably like to deny it, you're human and you have feelings, just like the rest of us. Sometimes, the hurt gets so bad, you feel like you want to curl up into a little ball and hide away someplace where no one can ever find you, where you never have to feel again or hurt again. But you can't hide forever. Believe me, I know. Sooner or later, you have to start living again. And you know what?"

"What?"

"Living isn't half bad."

"Sara?"

"Hmm?"

"I'm glad you came tonight."

"Me, too."

They lay quietly for a long time. A cool breeze rippled through the trees and over the open field. He felt her shiver beside him.

"Cold?"

"Mmm."

He drew her into his arms until her head rested on his shoulder and her sweetly scented hair pressed against his face.

"Thank you," she whispered, snuggling closer.

And for the first time in a long while, he felt an odd contentment steal over him as they watched the stars dance across the midnight sky.

THE CHIMES above the door announced Sara's entrance into Mrs. MacNamara's store. She stood just inside the doorway and took a quick glance around. The only person around was the man standing at the book rack, who seemed too engrossed in the first pages of a novel to even notice her. Mrs. MacNamara was nowhere to be seen.

Sara ran moist palms down the sides of her pink pantsuit, debating whether or not to make a run for it. It would be so easy to back out of the store and forget the whole thing. No one would even know that she'd been there.

No one, that was, except for the silver-eyed man sitting outside in his pickup truck right this very minute, ensuring she didn't chicken out. She'd told him to go about his business and she'd meet him back at the truck in a half hour. He had ignored her, coming around to open her door and help her out.

"Well?" she'd demanded.

"Well what?"

"Why don't you go to the post office or something? Or better yet, go across the street to the video store and get *Invasion of the Killer Turnips.*"

"No."

"No, you won't get *Killer Turnips* or no, you won't budge from here?"

"Both."

She had given him a hurt look. "Don't you trust me?"

He'd pinned her against the pickup and captured her mouth in a long, lazy kiss that had raised goose bumps on her skin and made the heat rush to her face. The man had no shame. He'd kissed her right in the middle of Main Street, leaving her too dazed to think clearly.

Then he'd drawled, "Not particularly."

She'd walked away on unsteady legs, mumbling to herself, and when she'd looked back, he'd been leaning against the truck, his arms folded in front of him, watching her.

There had been no turning back.

She retrieved a piece of paper from her jacket pocket and unfolded it. That was another thing. The man had an unhealthy attachment to list making. Grocery lists, lists of movies to rent, lists of things to do, and her least favorite, the one he'd titled simply "Combat Training." Her gaze slid down that particular scourge, past the items that had already been crossed off, and came to a halt at item number ten: Converse with a perfect stranger for at least five minutes.

"Well, hell," she muttered to herself.

Suddenly the door behind her opened and the musical tinkle of the bells swinging back and forth startled her into dropping the list. She picked it up, then realized that the man at the book rack had made his escape. She shrugged, deciding that it wasn't her fault there were no strangers around to accost. While she was here though, it only made sense to pick up some ice cream for dessert tonight.

Mrs. MacNamara was at the front counter, unpacking a carton of cigarettes and stocking the shelf behind her.

"Did you get any more ice cream in yet, Mrs. Mac?"

Mrs. MacNamara turned around with an indulgent smile. "Yes, dear. I stashed your favorite in the usual spot."

"Thanks! You're a lifesaver."

She had to crouch down and reach way to the back of the freezer, behind the TV dinners and the frozen vegetables to get at the ice cream. But even with her head in the freezer, she heard the muffled shouts followed by Mrs. MacNamara's startled cry.

Extricating herself from the freezer, Sara silently closed the door. Instinct told her to lay low as she turned to peer at the front of the store. Her stomach lurched when she saw the two youths, one fair and the other dark, standing in front of the counter, waving a couple of very real looking guns in Mrs. MacNamara's direction.

"Open the register and put the money in the bag," ordered the blond boy. "Now!" he demanded, his voice deep and menacing.

"Yeah," said the other one, "and throw in that carton

of smokes while you're at it. Make it quick, grandma. My trigger finger is getting real itchy."

Suddenly, he turned around and began scanning each aisle in turn, making his way slowly to the one where Sara was hiding. She held her breath as a cold, paralyzing shiver snaked up her spine. Her heart was beating double time and she could feel her body shaking with fear. His footsteps came closer, until she was sure he would spot her at any second.

"It's clear," he reported, and turned back.

"Go check the back room."

"Oh, come on, Kevin! I checked it the last time. It's your turn. I can handle it here."

"Just do what I tell you...."

While they argued, Sara looked over her shoulder to the entrance of the back room. It was less than two feet away. If only she could reach it without getting caught. She bit her lip. If she didn't try, she'd surely be caught anyway, as soon as one of them came back here. Glancing down the aisle one last time, she found that Kevin, the blond kid, had jumped over the counter and was emptying the till, while his accomplice held the gun on Mrs. MacNamara. It was the perfect opportunity and she slipped soundlessly into the back room, breathing a sigh of relief when she managed to escape.

Now what?

It would be easy enough just to walk out the back exit and call the police or alert Dakota. But that would mean leaving Mrs. MacNamara alone with armed punks and she wasn't about to let that happen.

She needed a plan and she needed it now.

Come on, Sara, she ordered herself, *think!* She desperately eyed the cluttered storeroom, her gaze falling on the large wooden desk in the corner. There was a phone up front, by the cashier, but none back here. Rifling through the drawers yielded nothing that she could use.

She looked around the room again, spotting the crates stacked against the back wall and prayed that they contained something useful, like baseball bats or toy guns. Anything that would give her the slightest advantage. She had nearly reached them when she tripped over something lying on the floor.

A crowbar. She picked it up, the iron rod heavy in her hand, and wondered how much force it would take to knock out one of the thickheaded idiots with this thing. In a few minutes, she would know. Opening her purse, she pulled out the sheaf of money she'd just withdrawn from the automatic teller machine and scattered the bills on top of the desk. Tossing down her purse, she positioned herself behind a shelf, hoping that whichever one of the young goons who came back here would be distracted enough by the money not to notice her sneaking up behind him. She took a deep, calming breath and willed her voice to sound normal.

"Mrs. Mac!" she called out. "I'm still counting the money to deposit today, but I can't find the bank book. Do you have a minute?"

There was a short silence before Mrs. MacNamara, her voice strained and edged with fear, said, "I'll be right there."

Sara tightened her grip on the crowbar and raised it above her head. She swallowed convulsively, her fingers clenching and unclenching on the cold metal rod. The action, in fact the entire situation, was strangely familiar, as if she'd lived it before. Suddenly, the memory crystallized and she smiled to herself. Of course the scenario was familiar—she'd written it! The details of the scene with Desiree came flooding back and Sara knew exactly what she had to do.

Loud footsteps echoed outside the door moments before one of the kids appeared on the threshold.

"Hot damn! We hit the jackpot, Kevin! There must be close to five hundred smackers here," he shouted, heading straight for the desk and carelessly putting down his gun as he bent to grab the cash.

She sneaked up behind him. By the time he turned to look for her, it was too late. She brought down the crowbar with all the strength she could muster and quickly took a step backward as he collapsed at her feet.

She screamed to cover up the thudding noise and quietly placed the crowbar on the floor. Then she deftly removed her jacket, grabbed the sleeve of her cotton blouse and ripped it at the seam. She also tore open a few buttons, pulled the edges of the blouse from her pants and tousled her hair.

"Don't touch me!" she yelled, reaching for the gun on the table. A Smith & Wesson .38. Perfect, she thought with a smile as her fingers closed around the butt.

"Oh, no! Please don't!" she shouted, biting down hard on her lips and wetting them with a flick of her tongue.

"Stop fooling around, Danny, and bring her out of there!"

Sara took a deep breath and let out another convincing scream before dashing out of the back room, one hand clutching her blouse together, the other held behind her back.

"Don't touch me, you beast!" she screamed, throwing a fearful glance across her shoulder. "Please don't shoot me. Just keep him away from me. Don't let him hurt me," she pleaded.

Taken by surprise, Kevin swung his gun around from a pale Mrs. MacNamara to Sara, then back again. His momentary confusion was all she needed and, in the blink of an eye, she had her gun aimed at him.

Sometimes, virginal theatrics came in quite handy.

The kid looked at her in stunned disbelief for a few moments before breaking into a wide grin.

"What do you think you're doing?"

Her gun trained on the boy, Sara felt an almost unnatural sense of calm invade her body, as though she'd stepped outside herself and the entire situation.

"Put the gun down, Kevin," she ordered quietly.

He snickered. "Or what? You gonna shoot me?"

She took a step closer to him. "That's a distinct possibility."

His smile disappeared. "Hold it right there," he yelled, showing the first signs of losing his cool. "Danny? Danny, come out here!"

"He's not coming."

"Don't come any closer. I mean it, or I'll off the old lady."

"I don't think so, Kevin," she said softly, "because I don't think you know how to use that very dangerous weapon you're waving around."

The gun, its safety lock still on, wavered ominously in Kevin's hand. "All I have to do is pull the trigger and the old woman is history. Don't push your luck, lady."

She continued as if he hadn't spoken, taking another step forward. "You pull that trigger and you'll be lucky not to shoot yourself in the foot. I, on the other hand, am an expert shot. Now we can do this the easy way and you can put the gun down, or I can make you put it down."

"I don't believe you."

"What don't you believe? That I'll pull the trigger? Or that I'll hit my target?"

"Neither. You're lying."

"Ah, Kevin—" she shook her head sadly "—I can see we're going to have to do this the hard way."

Keeping an eye on Kevin, she tightened her grip on the gun, aimed at her target and slowly squeezed the trigger.

9

"WHAT ON EARTH was that?" asked the customer standing beside Dakota.

"A gunshot," he answered flatly.

"Are you sure?" The sales clerk was doubtful. "It sounded like someone's car backfiring."

Dakota didn't bother explaining to the man that he knew the difference between the sound of a bullet leaving the barrel of a gun and exhaust coming out of a muffler. Instead, he turned and strode toward the door.

Dakota leaned against the frame, holding the door ajar with one foot. He took in the scene outside with a sweeping glance and straightened abruptly.

A small crowd had gathered on the sidewalk and he knew that whatever was going down, it was in Mrs. MacNamara's store. His gaze honed in on the beat-up Chevy sedan parked directly in front of his pickup. No one was inside, but the engine was still running and the rear plates were missing.

"Do you still want me to look for the *Invasion of the Killer Turnips*?" asked the harried store clerk.

"What I want you to do for me now is to call the police. Tell them MacNamara's convenience store is being held up," he said tersely, and left the video store.

Sara. That was the first thought that had popped into his mind, but he knew she was safe. She had to be. All she had to do in there was talk to a perfect stranger and come back out again. He knew how reluctant she had been, so she wouldn't have prolonged the torture. She was probably at the local craft store right now, picking out some wool, blissfully unaware of all the excitement.

Something in his gut tightened, but he ignored it, striding across the street to the idling Chevy. He opened the door, turned off the engine and pocketed the keys, then made his way to the pickup. He leaned against the side, waiting for Sara to come down the street and start nagging him into telling her what was going on.

He watched the crowd in front of him while he waited. A couple of kids were excitedly recounting what they had been able to see through the front window of the store.

"...a man holding up the store...wearing an army jacket and yelling..."

He scanned the street for any sign of Sara, his sense of unease growing.

"...woman in pink...clothes were torn...holding a gun, too..."

His breath caught in his lungs and he felt as if someone were twisting a knife inside him. It was some other woman in pink. It had to be. Where would Sara have found a gun?

But he knew. It was Sara in there, trapped with some homicidal maniac with a gun.

And knowing Sara, she'd probably provoked him into using it.

Dakota took a deep, labored breath. He was jumping to conclusions, acting worse than a rookie at boot camp. He was going to wait for the police to come. The first thing war had taught him was never to get involved. Not with the land, not with the cause and sure as hell not with the people. It clouded your judgment and got you killed, and if it didn't, it made moving on to the next assignment that much harder.

A second gunshot exploded from inside the store, and suddenly he was running, pushing his way through the crowd, trying to reach the door.

Fear clawed at him, ripping and tearing at his insides with razor-sharp talons. His dark nemesis terrified him because it threatened to unleash the deep emotions seething just under the surface of his skin and he didn't want to acknowledge them. *Not now. Damn, not now.*

In the end, it was white-hot fury that saved him. It erupted inside him in icy slivers of rage, manifesting itself in a cold, deadly sense of calm that cleared his mind and guided his actions. And the assailant backing up toward the front door was the target of his fury.

Dakota waited for the perfect moment, until the man was leaning on the door, pushing it open with his weight.

"You're crazy, lady! Do you know that? I'm getting outta here and you're not gonna stop me!"

"But I am," said Dakota as he pulled the door open, catching the man off guard and off balance. In the same moment, he reached for the man's hand, snapping the wrist bone with practiced ease.

The man howled in pain, and Dakota plucked the gun from his fingers. Before the assailant could run, Dakota had him pinned up against the wall by his throat.

A child, he thought, staring into the kid's terrified eyes. A child playing a deadly game.

"Dakota, please put him down."

Sara's voice. A little of his anger left him, replaced by a relief so profound, he shook with the force of it.

"If I were you, I'd thank the lady," he said softly. "She just saved your life."

The kid screamed an obscenity at him and Dakota released him with a certain measure of disgust. "Sit over by that wall and don't bother going anywhere. If I have to track you down, I might not be in such a forgiving mood."

The kid sat, cradling his wrist and whimpering. Dakota ignored him, checked the gun and turned his attention to Mrs. MacNamara.

"Are you okay, darlin'?"

She gave him a watery smile. "A bit too much excitement for my taste, but I'll live."

He smiled back at her and handed her the gun.

"If he moves, shoot him," he said, nodding to the kid before taking a deep breath and turning to face Sara for the first time since he'd entered the store.

She was a mess. Her blouse was torn, a few of the buttons were missing, her hair was mussed and sticking out all over the place, and she was staring at him as if she'd never seen him before.

He crossed the distance between them in a couple of strides and took the wavering gun from her hand. He checked it, put the safety lock on and stuffed it into the waistband of his jeans. Then he grabbed her chin and captured her lips in a crushing kiss. He devoured her mouth with all the urgency, the need, the *relief* inside him, plundering her soft warmth, stopping only when he ran out of breath.

She stared up at him with dazed brown eyes before gracing him with a brilliant smile. He had to stop himself from taking her mouth again and took her hand instead, pulling her toward the back room.

"Come with me," he ordered.

She stiffened and stopped, biting her lip.

"What's the matter?"

"I almost forgot about the one in the back. He's been out for an awfully long time. I hope I didn't kill him."

He was sure that nothing she could say would shock him anymore, sure that he'd become used to Sara's unpredictability.

He was wrong.

"There's another one?"

She nodded. "I lured him to the back and hit him over the head with a crowbar."

"And that's his gun you were waving around out there?"

"Uh-huh."

He closed his eyes and prayed for control.

They went into the back room and he checked the unconscious kid's pulse and breathing. Both were strong and steady, and Dakota had Mrs. MacNamara call an ambulance.

Finally, he straightened and turned to face her. "Sara, are you *crazy*?"

"I don't think so," she said carefully.

"Then just who the hell were you pretending to be out there? John Wayne and the Seventh Cavalry?"

"No, Desiree Miller, actually."

"Desiree." He kept his voice even. He wasn't going to strangle her. Not yet.

"Yes. There's this scene in *February in Freeport* where she lures one of the villains into the room and then knocks him out with a lead pipe. Then she—"

"You reenacted a scene out of one of your bloody spy novels?"

"Yes." A frown had settled on her face and she sounded distracted. "I've written hundreds of scenes like that—you know, those life-and-death ones—but I've never lived through one before. It never occurred to me how calm you become, how clear and focused everything seems, like you're looking at the world from outside yourself."

He took a deep, ragged breath. He knew exactly what she was talking about; he'd lived it all a hundred times. He'd felt the adrenaline pumping through his blood, felt the heady rush of power and then the deadly sense of calm as a life hung precariously in the balance. It was an addictive feeling, facing death and winning, and he didn't ever want Sara to become hooked.

"And if you'd shot yourself by accident, did you also think you were going to bleed ink?"

Her chin lifted. "I never shoot anything unless I aim to."

"Is that why you put a hole through the front door and blew that baby food jar to smithereens?"

"I was aiming at that jar."

"And the door?"

"I wanted to hit the chimes above the door, and I did. Unfortunately, they weren't enough to stop the impact of the bullet and it went through the glass."

He looked down at his boots and rubbed his neck tiredly.

"I'm an expert markswoman. I decided to take it up when I wrote my first book. Now I practice at a local shooting range." She shrugged and smiled. "They said I had a knack...."

"Shut up, Sara," he said through gritted teeth, reaching for her. "Just shut up and hold me."

She returned his embrace, her body trembling slightly and his arms tightened around her. He'd never felt anything remotely approaching the relief he felt now, holding Sara's soft, warm, *alive* body in his arms. He wanted to hold on and never let go.

He froze, wondering just what in Sam hell he was doing.

Getting involved. Becoming attached.

"Dakota?" she asked, her voice muffled against his chest.

"What?"

"Can I interest you in *Killer Turnips* and white chocolate chip ice cream tonight?"

No involvement. No commitment. No hassle.

"No!" He pulled away abruptly, running his shaking fingers through his hair.

"Dakota?" she asked again, sounding puzzled.

"No," he repeated, and walked out the door.

PERCHED ATOP a picnic table, her legs drawn to her chest, Sara sat facing the lake.

The sun had already sunk into the water, leaving a trail of blazing reds and oranges across the sky. Colorful fairy lights and Chinese lanterns, strung up early this morning for the town's Canada Day celebrations, twinkled gaily. Faint strains of music and laughter wafted on the balmy evening air. Bright bonfires lit the beach, the prime vantage point for watching the fireworks over the lake. Almost everyone had drifted there now and the picnic grounds, which had been teeming with people an hour ago, were practically deserted.

It was, she reflected, the first peaceful moment she'd found since yesterday afternoon. Soon after she'd followed Dakota out of the back room of Mrs. MacNamara's store, the ambulance, the police and the local newspaper reporter had arrived, followed by a throng of curious spectators. It seemed that everyone had started asking her questions all at once. She'd answered them as best she could, but after an hour of recounting the story repeatedly, she'd looked around in desperation for Dakota.

He'd been leaning against the front counter, arms folded across his chest in that now familiar stance, watching the scene with narrowed eyes. She'd sent him a pleading glance and, instantly, as if he'd been waiting for a signal from her, he'd straightened and taken over the situation with an ease that seemed born of long practice. Within minutes, the police and the reporter had been dispatched and the crowds cleared. He'd escorted her home in silence and accompanied her to the door. She'd asked him to come to the picnic today, but he'd declined politely and wished her a distant good-night before driving away.

She didn't blame him for being upset. It had been a foolish thing to do, confronting the robber like that. She'd realized it the moment Dakota had burst into the store. The savage look on his face had frightened her more than his anger. But when he'd finally turned to see her, the expression in his eyes—relief mixed with fear and something else she had been unable to identify—had melted her heart. In that moment, she'd felt like nothing else mattered except him, not her fears, not Parker, not anything. And when he'd kissed her...oh, when he'd kissed her, she'd known.

She was in love with him.

The tough, cynical image he projected was a cover for a man who was, in his own inimitable way, caring and protective. He'd threatened and bullied her into a lot of new experiences over the past two weeks and, in the process, she'd discovered a courage she never knew she'd possessed. He'd stepped back and allowed her to be independent, yet whenever she'd been faced with a *real* threat he'd been both possessive and protective of her.

The realization had been a dizzying one. This morning she'd woken up feeling happy and free and gloriously alive.

Like a whole new person.

A person who had the courage to walk into a bar, play pool and slow dance.

A person who had the courage to ride a Harley, kiss a man in public and foil a robbery attempt.

A person who had the courage to stop running and face her fears.

She'd spent most of the morning on the phone, making arrangements. First, a call to Kate explaining everything that had happened since they'd last talked and informing her of the new decisions she'd made. Next, a call to her agent to tell her that she was ready to do a book signing and, tentatively, the speech she'd been invited to give at a writers' convention in the fall.

The afternoon and most of the evening had been spent with Kate, manning the dessert table at the annual Beaver Creek Canada Day barbecue. It seemed that practically everyone in the entire county had stopped by the table at some point in the day to congratulate Sara for facing up to the two young robbers, but the only person she'd been interested in seeing was the one who hadn't shown up.

And as far as she was concerned, they had both waited long enough.

DAKOTA LEANED AGAINST the railing of the deck and stared out across the lake. He was easily able to make out the colorful lights and fires dotting the beach along the other side. Soon, they'd be starting the fireworks. He wondered if Sara enjoyed watching them as much as she liked watching the stars, wondered if her eyes and face would light up at the sight....

Damn it, he had to stop thinking about her.

He went inside to turn on the deck light, came back out and paced across the redwood planks. The restlessness had been plaguing him again all day. He'd thrust the feelings aside with ruthless efficiency while he'd been making arrangements for tomorrow, but now, in the glowing remnants of a summer twilight, they hounded him without reprieve.

He'd come outside hoping that the quiet music of the waves lapping against the shore and the gentle caress of the evening breeze would soothe the restless energy bottled up inside him. Instead, he'd been prowling around out here for a good half hour, unable to think of anything but Sara at the Canada Day picnic without him. She'd asked him to come yesterday, but he'd coolly informed her that he had some business to take care of. She'd seemed disappointed, her eyes losing some of their magical sparkle when he'd declined.

As soon as he got back home, he'd take up a good, solid vice to keep those great big brown eyes out of his head.

Damn inconsiderate woman.

He'd initially wanted only to stay long enough to get her into bed, but somewhere along the line, things had

changed. His feelings for Sara had changed. Her guts-
iness, her sweetness, her sense of humor made him ad-
mire her as a person, not just as an object of his desire.

And therein lay the danger. Whenever he contem-
plated his complete and utter loss of control yesterday,
he broke out in a cold sweat. The tight rein he usually
kept over his emotions had collapsed under the weight
of his fear for Sara. And he hadn't liked the feeling, not
one bit.

That was the reason he was leaving for home tomorrow. He had no desire to become any more involved
with Sara than he already was because, in the end,
she'd be the one to get hurt.

As for their deal, well, he'd fulfilled his part. Just
yesterday, she had mastered all the tasks on her list.
Besides, there was no doubt in his mind that any one of
the men at The Honky Tonk, including Jacko, the soft-
hearted sot, would be more than happy to escort her to
the party. But he had a feeling she was going to pick
Evan and if she wanted to take a man who was going
to suffocate her on the dance floor, that was fine with
him.

Disturbing images of Sara and Evan flashed through
his brain and he cursed, shoving his hands through his
hair in frustration.

No, damn it, it wasn't fine. *He* wanted to be the one
holding her enticingly curved body in his arms. *He*
wanted to be the one kissing her, savoring the delicious, delicate taste of her. And more than anything
else in the whole world, he wanted to be inside her,
making hot, sweet love to her.

With a ragged groan, he closed his eyes, imagining
her before him, her soft, gentle fingers touching him,
stroking and caressing his hardness....

"Dakota?"

Slowly, he opened his eyes at the whispered question, wondering if the intensity of his longing had somehow conjured her up. He caught the sweet scent of wildflowers that hung in the air and knew that she was as real as the hot desire pulsing through his blood.

Sara stared at him, strangely fascinated by the burning intensity of his smoky gaze fixed upon her face. A slow, familiar heat began to unfurl in her belly and radiate outward, weakening her knees and sending tiny shivers exploding throughout her body. Just as her breath began coming in short, erratic spurts, he looked away.

"You shouldn't have come here, Sara." His voice was warm and husky with need.

She reached out gentle fingers to caress the hard curve of his jaw. "I had to. I need to tell you something."

His skin was warm and rough beneath her fingertips as she lightly traced them over the sculpted features of his face, his jaw, his cheeks, his lips, until he stepped back, out of reach.

"Don't you want to know what it is?"

"No," he said on a strangled groan.

"Too bad." She closed the distance between them, trapping him against the railing, and pressed her body intimately against his, until she heard his sharply drawn breath. "Because—"

"Don't do this."

"—I've decided—"

"Sara—"

"—that I want you."

"Damn it all, woman."

"That wasn't quite the reaction I was hoping for."

"You don't know what you're doing, Sara."

"I know exactly what I'm doing," she murmured, sliding her arms around his neck. "I'm not running anymore."

"Have I ever told you that you have lousy timing?"

She planted feathery kisses along the strong, tanned column of his throat, stopping at the place where his pulse jerked rapidly under her lips. "Is that your way of telling me you're not chasing me anymore?"

"Yes."

She smiled at the hoarse desperation in his voice. "It's going to take a lot more than words to persuade me. It's going to take proof," she said, tightening her grip around his waist and leaning into the rigid length of him. "And I can feel some hard evidence right now that says you're lying."

"It's an automatic reaction for a man to be aroused by a woman."

"Not just any woman. Me," she said.

"Me and my big mouth," he muttered.

"I happen to think it's a very sexy mouth. Now shut up and put it to good use."

"Sara, there's something I need to tell you, too. I—"

She silenced him by pressing a soft kiss against his lips. For one endless, breathless moment, he resisted.

Then he was hauling her toward him and kissing her, deeply, slowly, thoroughly, ravishing her mouth, robbing her of breath and strength, until she leaned against him, limp and aching. Wordlessly, he swung her into his arms and deposited her gently on the cushioned lounger on the grass nearby, carefully lowering his weight on her. She moaned in pleasure, reveling in the feel of his hard, lean body on hers.

"Dakota..." His name on her lips was a sigh and a plea tangled together.

He stared into her eyes, his own deep and dark and filled with smoky desire. "Tell me what you want."

Slowly, holding his gaze with her own, she took his hands and brought them to the buttons of her shirt. "You," she whispered.

One by one, he released the buttons while she held her breath, her pulse skittering out of control every time his fingers grazed her skin. Finally, he parted the white cotton and unhooked the clasp on the front of her bra. She saw his hands shake as he set aside the lacy folds.

"Sara," he breathed, staring at her. "I've imagined you like this so many times since that first night, all white and creamy and beautiful."

He cupped a breast in one large hand and kneaded the ripe mound, flicking a pink tip with his thumb. "So perfect."

She moaned, arching beneath his touch as the heat began to uncoil and spread from the burgeoning nipple to all the soft, secret, womanly places inside her.

"And so responsive," he murmured, bending to capture the swollen bud in his mouth.

She cried out as he took her inside him, the damp, insistent tugging of his mouth flooding her with warmth and piercing waves of hot desire.

"You taste so good," he whispered. "So hot and sweet and sexy."

He turned his attention to the other nipple, caressing and sucking until she clung to him, mindless with pleasure, her loud cries echoing in the dark stillness of the night.

"A screamer," he murmured with a smile.

Her fingers tangled in his dark mane as she held him to her and gasped, "I suppose...if you're embarrassed...we can take it inside."

"Nothing about you embarrasses me, love," he said, trailing soft, wet kisses back to her mouth.

"That's good, because I really don't care to move right now."

Her hands went to his chest and she began to unbutton his shirt, dragging it off his shoulders. She stared in fascination at the gleaming, rippling mass of bronzed skin and hard muscle before reaching out to run her hands lovingly across its width, feeling the warmth of his flesh, the thud of his heart beating, the roughness of the crisp, dark hairs. This was what she had missed the last time they had made love, this tactile, sensual exploration of him.

"You feel good. Hard and warm and furry," she said, bending to trail her tongue across his heated skin, tasting the salty tang of him, stopping to lave one hard, flat nipple, then the other.

Dakota closed his eyes briefly, feeling her delicate fingers skim over his chest, feeling her mouth on him, and let out a ragged breath. He was sure he'd never been so hard or ached so much in his entire life, and he didn't know how much longer he could go on like this, having her in his arms without losing complete control. She was soft and warm and so achingly beautiful. Her face was flushed with passion, her lips swollen and pink from his kisses. For the second time in two days, he found himself in the grip of an emotion so powerful, he was helpless to resist. And then he looked into her eyes, rich and golden brown and trusting, and he knew he had to make the effort; she deserved better than what he had to offer.

"We can't go further. I won't be able to stop."

"I don't want you to stop."

"Sara..."

She stroked his cheek, her fingers cool on his heated skin, and stared into his eyes, her own soft and dark. "Make love to me, Dakota."

Her quiet plea unleashed something raw and powerfully primitive deep in his gut, something dark and hungry and needy, yet infinitely tender and fiercely protective. Brushing a thumb across the ripe fullness of her lips, he parted the velvety petals before claiming them in a gentle kiss.

A warm mingling of breaths, a soft whispering of lips, it was the sweetest kiss he had ever given her, filled with a simple eroticism that made her heart and body ache with longing. She closed her eyes as he trailed kisses down her jaw and neck and breasts, his mouth hot on her skin, his hair cool and silky under her fingers. His warm palms slid over her stomach to the waistband of her jeans. She heard the scrape of a zipper opening and then his thick voice commanding, "Lift your hips, honey."

She obeyed, allowing him to smooth her jeans and panties down her hips and legs, and then she was naked beneath his gaze.

For a long, long moment he took in his fill of her. She fought the urge to cover herself up with her hands as his smoldering gaze traveled down the length of her with slow deliberation, skimming her shoulders and breasts, tracing over her stomach and hips, lingering on her thighs and legs.

And then he touched her.

Slowly. Exquisitely. Reverently.

His lips scorched her body, his hands seared her

skin, his body branded her as his. And when she thought she'd die from the pleasure of it, he began all over again, teasing, tasting, tantalizing until she burned for him.

"Dakota...!"

"Slow." His mouth was hot against her skin as he trailed wet, openmouthed kisses up her inner thigh. "This time, we're going to take it...nice and slow."

"Please..." She arched her hips and opened her legs wider, inviting him to touch her in that one, intimate place where all the wickedly wanton sensations he'd aroused in her had pooled with delicious urgency.

He seemed to understand her need perfectly because in the next instant she was crying out, gripping a fistful of grass in each hand as his tongue flicked out to tease the tiny, sensitive morsel of flesh that she offered him. And when his mouth closed fully over her, she thought she'd go out of her mind.

But she needed more. She needed to feel the hard length of him against her, inside her.

"I want you inside me," she whispered.

For a moment, she thought he hadn't heard her, then he lifted his head and groaned, moving to cover her body with his and capturing her mouth in a deep, intoxicating kiss.

Frantically, she reached down and undid his belt, his zipper, and slid down his jeans and his briefs. He throbbed, hot and hard and heavy under her hand.

Lightly, she stroked the length of him, marveling when his breath caught and he moaned deep in his throat.

"Don't, sweetheart, don't," he whispered unsteadily. "I won't be able to control myself."

She watched as he turned away for a moment to

shed his clothes and protect her with a condom and then their mouths and tongues and skin were melting into each other, until she could no longer distinguish their separate beings, could only feel the achingly sweet sensations that came from the fusion of flesh against hot flesh.

"Dakota, please. I need you so much."

"I know," he said, rubbing against her with maddening slowness. "Ah, love, you're ready for me, aren't you?"

She ground herself against him in a wild frenzy, aching for something more, something just beyond her grasp.

She felt the tip of his shaft nudge her opening and then he was inside her, stretching her, filling her and she was falling, tumbling freely, gloriously over the edge into release. He captured her scream of joy with a kiss, murmuring soothing words of comfort against her lips as his hips rocked her gently back and forth, moving with slow, deep strokes, bringing her unbelievably back to that dizzying precipice. She lifted her hips, instinctively wrapping her legs around his flanks, her fingers digging into his back as he sank deeper into her. Opening her eyes, she saw him poised above her, his eyes closed, his head flung back, his back arched, the strong, corded muscles of his neck straining as he fought for control.

"Let go, darling," she urged, reaching up to touch the harsh, raw-boned beauty of his face. "Let go."

He cried out as the full force of his passion engulfed him, plunging harder, deeper, building her pleasure, taking her higher, further, until she spiraled out of orbit again, clutching his shoulders as the world tilted precariously for a moment before giving way under her. Seconds later, she heard him gasp, felt his body shudder violently before he collapsed on top of her.

FOR A LONG WHILE, Dakota lay utterly still, concentrating simply on dragging the air back into his lungs. When his heart no longer thundered in his chest and the blood no longer roared in his ears, he became aware of other things. Cool fingers lightly caressing his back. Warm lips raining soft kisses on his shoulder. Small, slim arms wrapped tightly around his middle. Smooth, silky legs tangled around his. The deep contentment that filled him.

He opened his eyes and found her staring up at him, her eyes wide and shimmering with tears. A shaft of remorse pierced through him as they spilled onto her cheeks. He hadn't meant to lose control like that again.

"Sara..." he whispered, bending to capture the salty droplets with his tongue. "I'm sorry if I hurt you."

A slow smile lit her face and he caught his breath at the sheer beauty of it. "You didn't." And then her eyes took on a naughty twinkle. "That was quite a performance, Mr. Wilder. I, uh, think you brought the house down."

He followed her gaze down the side of the lounger, belatedly realizing that the legs had collapsed and that they were considerably closer to the ground now than when they had begun.

"Damn."

Laughter bubbled from her lips. "I think we'll have to find something sturdier next time."

He kissed her softly and tried to ease his weight from her.

Her arms tightened around him. "Can we stay out here a little longer? I'd like to see the fireworks."

He shifted slightly, until she was lying on top of him, and gathered her up in his arms. "Honey, we've already experienced the best kind."

She laughed and nestled closer. "Dakota?"

"Hmm?"

"Do you think the neighbors heard us?"

He grinned, rubbing his cheek against her hair. "Probably."

"Do you think they'll be terribly shocked?"

"Oh, terribly."

"Good," she said with considerable satisfaction, dropping a kiss on his shoulder and yawning.

A few minutes later, she asked again, "Dakota?"

"What, honey?"

"I love you," she murmured drowsily. And then she curled up against him like a contented kitten and sighed, her lashes fluttering shut.

10

FOR A LONG, long while, he simply stared at her. Even when the night sky burst into a kaleidoscope of dazzling color and light, he couldn't tear his eyes away from the woman sleeping so peacefully in his arms.

"Damn," he whispered finally.

What the hell had he done? He never should have let this happen, never should have let his hunger for her overpower his self-control again. He was thirty-three years old for God's sake, not a horny teenager tasting sex for the first time. Surely he could have resisted just a few more hours? But...she'd been so sweet, so irresistibly warm and giving... He hadn't been able to withstand the temptation.

And now she thought she was in love with him.

He looked down at her, slumbering so trustingly against him, her skin glowing in the starlight, her fingers loosely curled in his chest hair, her pink lips parted slightly. Something tightened in his chest. She deserved so much better, deserved a man who could give her all the promises and declarations a woman like Sara needed. She deserved someone who could give her forever; he didn't believe in forever.

"I'm sorry, baby," he said softly, tenderly smoothing a lock of damp hair from her forehead.

She sighed and snuggled closer. He held her a while

longer, until the breeze from the lake turned cool and he could no longer put off what needed to be done.

SARA STIRRED SLOWLY, gradually becoming aware that the mattress under her was too firm to be her own, and that the warm comfort that had enveloped her throughout the night was gone. It was a struggle, but she finally managed to open her eyes to an unfamiliar room bathed in the dim glow of a small table lamp. A shadowed figure stood by the bed, strangely silent and still.

"Dakota?" she asked, squinting at him in confusion.

"I'm here."

She smiled and stretched languidly as memories of the previous evening came flooding back, then winced when she felt the slight soreness that had invaded her body during the night.

"Sara?" His voice was filled with concern. "Are you all right?"

"I'm fine," she reassured him with a rueful grin that turned into a huge yawn.

He turned away from her, making his way to the dresser. "Go back to sleep."

She struggled into a sitting position, clutching the covers to her chest and watching him with shy pleasure. He wore a pair of faded jeans and very little else, leaving the bronzed expanse of his back exposed to her hungry gaze. The powerful muscles rippled as he opened a drawer and took out a T-shirt. He pulled it over his head and began stuffing the hem into the waistband of his jeans. Frowning, she noted that his hair was still wet, as if he'd just taken a shower.

Puzzled, she asked, "What time is it?"

He picked up his boots and sat down in a chair. "Five."

"How come you're up so early? It's not even light out yet."

He finished pulling on his boots and stood, finally turning to face her, his expression blank. A cold sense of foreboding trickled up her spine. "What's wrong?"

"I have to leave for Zaire in a couple of hours."

She was immediately concerned. "Is there something wrong at the mine? Not another explosion? Is it Loch? Has something happened to him?"

"There's nothing wrong. Loch is fine."

She stared at him in bewilderment. "Then I...I don't understand."

His face was stone-cold, and his eyes were frosted silver as he stared down at her. "There's nothing to understand. I'm leaving to go back home today. Now. I tried to tell you yesterday, but—"

But she'd been too busy seducing him to listen.

"What...what about the party?"

He smiled thinly. "I'm sure that if you ask real nicely, one of your honky-tonk cowboys will be more than happy to escort you."

She bit her lip to keep it from trembling. "I see."

"We had a deal, Sara."

She bent her head and stared at her white knuckled fingers clutching the navy blue coverlet.

"You knew I'd be leaving sooner or later."

Yes, she'd known. But last night, after he'd made love to her and held her, she'd foolishly allowed herself to dream. She had dreamed that she meant something to him and that he would ask her to go back to Africa with him.

She swallowed, her throat tight and raw with an

emotion that threatened to choke her. "We made love last night," she whispered.

"No, Sara. We had sex. Don't confuse it with something it wasn't," he said harshly.

"All right. I made love and you had sex. It doesn't change the fact that I still love you."

For the first time that morning, his mask slipped and his silver eyes blazed fire. "No, goddamn it, you don't!"

She flinched at his vehemence, and sat silently as he turned away with a sound of frustration and shrugged into his jacket.

When he turned to face her once again, his eyes were implacably cold. "Haven't you figured it out yet, sweetheart? Why do you think I was interested in a woman like you in the first place? Why do you think I tried to help you?"

"I...I thought..."

"You thought I'd been a sucker for a pair of brown eyes and a smile?" His own smile was cold as he picked up a suitcase from the foot of the bed. "Wrong again. I keep telling you, you've got to stop being so naïve. The truth is, you asked for it and I obliged."

His hand was on the doorknob when she whispered, "Dakota?"

He stopped on the threshold.

Her heart lurched painfully.

"So long, babe. Don't forget to lock up on your way out."

And he was gone.

For a long time afterward, Sara sat, dry-eyed and shivering on the cold, empty bed while something inside her slowly shriveled up and died.

THE WORDS in front of her rippled and blurred like a desert mirage, then broke apart and finally faded altogether.

Lifting her glasses from the bridge of her nose, Sara pressed her fingers to her eyes for a long moment. She'd been staring at the screen far too long, but she couldn't stop. Not now. Writing, page after page after word-filled page, was an odd kind of therapy. She found that, as long as she concentrated on finishing *July in Jerusalem,* as long as she concentrated on dreaming up the best, most painful ways of punishing the Jaguar, she could contain the rage bubbling just under the surface of her skin.

It hadn't been long in coming. The numbness had worn off after the first day and then an unholy fury had begun to build inside her. The result of that fury was in the envelope currently propped up against the printer. Once, she'd picked it up and nearly sent it. But the strange tightness in her chest, the hard lump in her throat and the knifing pain in her heart had stopped her. Somewhere, deep inside, she knew that if she sent it, she'd have to face the fact that her relationship with Dakota was over, once and for all. She wasn't ready for that. So she kept writing. And if her eyes burned and her body ached, well, at least her agent would be happy. She replaced her glasses and began doggedly to type once again.

The phone rang a few times. She ignored it and kept typing.

The doorbell rang. Once, twice, three times. She typed faster.

When the pounding began, she tried to ignore that too, but it wouldn't go away, becoming louder and more furious by the minute.

She stood and stalked to the front door, muttering under her breath, "Damn interruptions! How am I supposed to get any work done?"

Flinging open the door, she glared at her visitor. "What do you want?"

"You look like hell run over," said Kate as she stepped inside. "Twice."

Sara slammed the door shut. "Great. Now that you've complimented me, please feel free to leave. I've got work to do."

Kate ignored her and walked into the living room. She settled herself comfortably on the sofa with all the appearance of laying a lengthy siege.

Sara clenched her jaw. "Did you hear me? I have work to do."

"Yes, I heard. I'm not deaf. I'm ignoring you."

"I have a deadline."

"Congratulations," was Kate's dry rejoinder to that subtle hint.

"Kate!"

"Honey, you might as well resign yourself. I'm not moving until you tell me exactly what's been going on here. First Dakota Wilder hightails it out of town faster than you can say 'coward' and then you regress back to hermit mode. What gives?"

Sara turned around and walked into the kitchen. "What do you want to drink? Coffee, iced tea or lemonade?"

"I didn't come for lemonade. I came to make sure you were all right. You haven't been answering your calls."

"I'm letting the machine get them. I've been too busy to be bothered."

"For three days? Day and night?"

"Yes," she said defiantly. "You know how I am when I'm writing." She tried for a laugh. It came out short and brittle.

"Yes, I believe I do." Kate's voice was thoughtful as she joined Sara in the kitchen. "You made love with him again, didn't you?"

"No, Kate, we had sex again," she said matter-of-factly, searching for a clean glass. "It was a good, standard lay, I believe, but nothing too earth-shattering. And then he left. Sure I can't get you something to drink?"

"I was afraid of that."

"I'm sorry, would you rather have something to eat?" She opened the fridge and poked her head inside. "I think I have some bread and cheese, though it might have gone moldy by now. It was someplace around here—"

"Sara, come out of there, please."

She straightened and closed the refrigerator door with a frown. "Maybe I can dig up a can of something from the cupboard—"

"Sara, honey, please talk to me."

"Don't prod, Kate."

"How can I not prod?" cried Kate. "Look at you! Just look at what you've done to yourself. How long has it been since you've slept? Since you've eaten a decent meal or stepped outside?"

Sara carefully put the glass down and gripped the counter with desperate fingers.

"My God," continued Kate, "it's as if the last two weeks had never happened."

Sara closed her eyes. She wished they'd never happened, wished she'd never laid eyes on that dark-haired, silver-eyed stranger that night at Billy Joe's.

The old hurt with Parker was nothing, *nothing*, compared with the slashing pain that was slicing through her now, a piercing reminder of the foolishness of abandoning well-grounded fears.

Why did you think I was interested in a woman like you in the first place?

"Honey, I know you're hurting right now, but you—"

"Hurting?" Sara whirled around to face her friend. "I'm not hurting. I'm furious! Do you hear me? *Furious!*"

"You have every right to be angry at him—"

"You don't understand. I'm angry at *myself*, Kate, for letting my guard down even for a minute. I knew this was going to happen. I *knew* it and I still let myself fall in love with him."

"How could you have known?"

"Because men don't fall in love with women like me," she said flatly. "Parker taught me that. It was a painful lesson and you would think I'd know better, but I let myself forget. I got caught up in the fantasy, believed he could love me back, just because I wanted to believe it so badly."

"It wasn't a fantasy, honey. Don't you see? It happened and because of it, you're a different person."

"Funny, I don't feel a whole lot different from the last time I got dumped," said Sara sarcastically.

"Did you or did you not tell me last week that you felt like a whole new person?" demanded Kate. "Can you honestly say that you would have set one foot over a Harley a month ago? Played pool with a bunch of cowboys? Gone off looking at the stars in the middle of the night? Stopped a robbery in progress? Slept with a man?"

Sara remained stubbornly silent.

Kate strode back into the living room, snatched up her purse, and slung it over her shoulder. "Fine, don't answer me. You can sit here inside your safe little cottage for the rest of your life, hiding away and feeling sorry for yourself. But just remember one thing. Inside that grubby robe, behind those awful glasses and underneath that rat's nest of hair is the real Sara Matthews. And if you have a lick of sense, you'll let her out, go to that damn party next Saturday and show everyone exactly what she's made of."

Sara watched mutely as Kate walked to the front door and opened it.

"Kate?"

Kate stopped on the threshold. "Yeah?"

"Don't you dare leave without telling me what I should wear."

A slow smile spread across Kate's face. "That's easy. Something sexy. Think provocative. Think alluring. Think seductive."

"Think again. This is my parents' anniversary."

"Leave it up to me, honey. We've got more than a week till D day and in that time, I'm going to make you into a whole new woman," said Kate, making for the door again.

"Where are you going?"

"Into town to pick up some fashion mags."

"Would you do me a favor? Mail something on your way?"

DAKOTA PICKED UP the unassuming white envelope from his desk and turned it around in his fingers. He'd been staring at the neatly printed return address on the upper left corner for the better part of an hour. He wondered why he was so reluctant to open it, then admitted to himself that it was because he didn't really want to know what Sara had to say to him. He'd been such a bastard that morning that the last thing he'd been expecting from her was a letter.

A bullet between the eyes was more her style.

"Damn it, Wilder, what the hell's the matter with you?"

He looked up, dropping the unopened envelope into his desk drawer, and coolly raised a questioning brow at the tall, well-built man who had just stormed into his office.

"Aside from the fact that you've just shattered my eardrums? Not a whole hell of a lot."

"Ever since you came back over a week ago, you've done nothing but sit in this airless closet and work."

"I'm assuming you're complaining?" he drawled.

"Yes, damn your stubborn hide, I'm complaining. And don't give me any of this bull about catching up on work, either. You know Jesse did a great job while you were gone."

"Yeah, Jesse did great while I was gone, but unless he's planning to permanently replace me, I believe I still have a job to do."

Loch ran a hand through his sizzling crop of red hair. "It's just not like you," he muttered.

Dakota lifted the other brow.

Loch threw him a sheepish look. "You know I didn't mean it that way."

"I sincerely hope not."

"Look, all I'm trying to say is that you're never happy unless you're outside, talking to the miners and their wives or harassing the bureaucrats and making sure everything is running smoothly. It's not like you to spend more than an hour at a time cooped up in here. Lately though, you've been coming in at dawn and not leaving this damn stuffy office until past midnight."

Dakota didn't bother telling Loch that he hadn't gone home last night. What was there to go home to except emptiness? His whole life seemed to stretch out before him, emptier and lonelier than ever.

"You haven't even been to The Canteen to shoot any pool since you got back. The guys have been asking about you. Hell, even Big Eddie misses you. Says he hasn't had a challenging game since you went away. Why don't you drop by tonight?"

Dakota sat back and ran a tired hand across his jaw. "I'm not in the mood."

He wasn't in the mood for much these days. Probably because everything he did reminded him of Sara. When he thought of going out and shooting a game, he'd picture Sara leaning over the pool table at The Honky Tonk, cue stick in hand, her face lighting up with a smile as she pocketed her first ball.

The woman was driving him crazy.

He couldn't go outside and look at the stars without remembering the night he'd shared them with her and wishing she was beside him again. He couldn't sleep without imagining her in his arms, soft and warm and lovely, and thinking about the magical night they'd shared under the stars. Always when he remembered that night, he became hard and ached for her and then he'd remember the morning after. The pleading look in her eyes, the thread of hope tangled with bewilderment in her voice the last time she'd said his name, and, finally, her eyes as they'd been when he'd left her. Somehow, he couldn't shake the feeling that he'd killed something fragile and infinitely precious that morning.

He kept telling himself that he'd done it for her own good. He knew better than anyone how foolish it was to become attached to people. They rewarded your love by running away or dying on you and then you were left with nothing except a desperate loneliness.... No, he'd done the right thing by ending it, before she'd become any more attached and before he'd fallen—

"Damn it, Wilder, snap out of it! Hell, this is worse than the last time," muttered Loch. "Listen, you've got to do something about your woman trouble. You're driving us all crazy around here."

"The feeling is mutual."

"If I didn't know better, I'd think you were lovesick."

Dakota pierced Loch with a killing glare. "Then it's a good thing you do know better, isn't it?"

Slowly, a big grin spread across Loch's face and his blue eyes filled with suppressed laughter. "I don't believe this. Don't tell me, she flashed her sweet little smile and you fell flat on your backside."

"If you're done with the stand-up routine, get the hell out of my office and let me get back to work."

"Call her and put us all out of our misery."

"The door is behind you. Use it."

"Man, you've got it bad."

Dakota flung a crude epithet at Loch, who ignored it and strolled out of the office, still grinning. As soon as the door closed behind his friend, Dakota ran trembling fingers through his hair.

Lovesick.

The realization struck him with the force of a hammer blow to the head, shattering all the twisted beliefs he'd ever held about love; the pieces came raining down around him, rearranging themselves into a truth that astounded him with its clarity.

It was already too late not to become attached because, whether he liked it or not, he was head over bloody boots in love. He'd been too stupid, too cowardly to admit it until now because admitting it, even to himself, would mean risking the pain and hurt of rejection if Sara ever decided to leave him. But if he never took that risk, he would condemn himself to a lifetime without love, without Sara's smile, without her laughter. A lifetime of loneliness.

Reaching into the drawer, he pulled out Sara's letter. For a long time, he stared at it. Finally, with careful precision, he slit open the top with a letter opener and lifted out a check. It was made out for a familiar sum and stuck on top of it was a small yellow note. It read simply, "For services rendered."

He leaned back in his chair, his lips slowly curving into a small, deadly smile.

SARA STOOD at the bottom of the steps leading to the entrance of her parents' house and tried to quell the feeling of dread the massive oak doors roused in the pit of her stomach.

She was late. Not just a few minutes tardy, but an entire two hours late.

And she was alone. Unescorted. Dateless.

Closing her eyes, she tried to convince herself that her cowardly days were over. But her legs weren't paying attention. They were too busy quaking underneath the floating layers of black chiffon and her heart was too busy hammering beneath the tight-fitting strapless bodice.

She remembered the last time she'd felt this way. It was at The Honky Tonk, and she remembered the way Dakota had offered her his hand, his touch a strong, silent anchor in a sea of fear. How she wished she was with him now, her cold fingers nestled in the warm comfort of his.

A sharp pain speared her heart and she clutched desperately at her evening bag. She had to stop thinking about him. Dakota Wilder was a part of her past; she'd seen to that when she'd asked Kate to mail that check for her. It had been her way of saying goodbye, of letting him know that, as far as she was concerned, their relationship had been nothing more than a simple business transaction.

In other words, it had been an open invitation to be struck down by lightning. Sara glanced quickly up at the clear evening sky, breathed a sigh and started up the stairs.

She had to go on with her life and, like it or not, she was on her own tonight. Somehow, she'd have to find the courage to get through it alone.

THE HOUSE was the same, glittering jewel bright under the crystal chandeliers and tasteful decorations. The people, her parents' friends and business associates, were the same, decked out in tuxes and designer ballgowns, laughing, talking, mingling with an air of carefully cultivated gaiety. The music, the food, the conversation, they were all the same. There was only one difference.

This time, Sara was actually enjoying herself.

She'd walked into the ballroom ten minutes ago, her head held high and a smile on her lips. It was incredible what an air of self-confidence could accomplish.

Whereas once people had treated her as though she were one of the gleaming white marble columns, now they smiled and nodded politely. Someone had even kindly grabbed a glass of champagne from a passing waiter for her. She took a sip now, grimaced as the bubbles tickled her nose, and put the glass down on a table as she walked by it.

Of course, it helped that no one had recognized her yet. Kate had insisted on a "girls' weekend out" in the big city and the two of them had ended up at an exclusive designer salon in trendy, upscale Yorkville for a complete makeover. As a result, Sara had acquired a short, sophisticated new haircut, extended wear contact lenses and a whole new wardrobe which, according to Kate, "screamed" sexy, confident celebrity author.

The transformation, it seemed, was successful. For the moment, she was one of them, just another guest. The real test would come when she found her parents. Scanning the crowded room, she spotted her mother's dark hair in the middle of a small cluster of older women. As she slowly neared the group, her mother turned and sent her a polite smile. Seconds later, the smile froze on her lips and her brown eyes widened in surprise.

"Sara?"

Well, at least her own mother recognized her, she thought ruefully, leaning over to place a kiss on a well-powdered cheek.

"Happy anniversary, Mother."

"I... Thank you, dear," said Mrs. Matthews faintly. "Ladies, you remember my daughter, Sara?"

A polite chorus of affirmatives reverberated around Sara, tagged on the tail end by a seemingly disembodied voice demanding, "You mean the one who's finally bringing home a fella?"

Sara couldn't help it. She laughed.

The smile Mrs. Matthews gave Sara was pained. "Yes, Elise, that's the one."

"Well, move out of my way and let me get a look at her," commanded the disgruntled voice. "She can't be all that bad if she had the good sense to throw over that slimy, good-for-nothing Jackson boy you and Kenneth are so fond of."

"Elise, please!"

The woman who finally emerged from behind two others was a tiny, bejeweled dynamo with bright auburn hair and twinkling blue eyes.

Sara recognized her as an L. A. Michaels fan who had been at the book signing this afternoon.

"Hello, Mrs. Stevenson."

The woman's eyes widened as she stared at Sara in awe. "It's you! But... Good heavens, Elizabeth," she said, turning accusing eyes on Sara's mother, "I'm going to strangle you! You said she scribbled for a living. Scribbled!"

"Well, yes, of course she does," began Mrs. Matthews.

"But she's L. A. Michaels!" exclaimed Mrs. Stevenson.

A shocked murmur echoed from the other ladies in the group.

Sara took one look at her mother's bewildered face and decided to take pity on her. "I'm afraid I asked her to keep it quiet until we were ready to announce it officially, Mrs. Stevenson."

Mrs. Stevenson sent Elizabeth Matthews a grudging look of forgiveness before turning to the others. "You should have seen the lineup, girls. Hundreds of people. I had to wait for over an hour to get my brand-new copy of *June in Jakarta* signed."

"I'm sorry for the inconvenience," Sara apologized. "We had a larger turnout than we expected."

Which was why she'd all but spent her next royalty check trying to bribe the taxi driver into sprouting wings on the way here.

"I'd like to send you an autographed copy of my next book to make up for the inconvenience," she offered.

Elise Stevenson beamed. "That would be lovely, my dear. I can hardly wait to get my hands on it. That Jon McAllister is such a stud puppy!"

"Elise!"

"Oh, lighten up, Lizzie!" Mrs. Stevenson dismissed Elizabeth Matthews and turned back to Sara. "How on earth do you come up with all those nasty situations to put Jon into? Poor man. Thank goodness he has Desiree to rescue him...."

For the next few minutes, Sara found herself in the middle of an enthusiastic bunch of L. A. Michaels fans who somehow managed to thwart her mother's every attempt to get her alone and question her about her missing date. Finally, Mrs. Matthews politely but firmly took Sara's arm and drew her aside.

"Well?"

"Well what?"

"Where is he?" demanded Mrs. Matthews, peering expectantly over Sara's shoulder. "I've been dying to meet—" She broke off suddenly, her eyes widening in shock. "Good Lord!"

"What is it, Mother? Are you all right?"

"I..."

"Pay her no mind, dear," Mrs. Stevenson said, coming up behind Sara's mother. "I have to admit to being a little speechless myself when I first saw him."

"Who?"

"The hunka-hunka burnin' love who just entered the ballroom."

Sara made a move to turn around just as Mrs. Stevenson hissed, "Ssh. And don't everyone turn around at once. The lot of you will scare him away." Mrs. Stevenson pinned Elizabeth Matthews with her shrewd gaze. "All right, Lizzie. Out with it. Who is he?"

"I don't know," said Mrs. Matthews with a frown.

"It's your party. You're supposed to know everyone here."

"I do. I did. The only person I haven't met yet is Sara's escort, whom, I might add, she was in the process of telling me about before you so rudely interrupted, so if you don't mind—"

"He's coming this way!"

Sara watched in amazement as her mother's hand flew up to pat an imaginary strand of hair in place.

"Doesn't *anybody* know who he is?"

"What if he's a party crasher?"

"Oh, my. He's looking at me!"

Mrs. Matthews sniffed elegantly. "Don't flatter yourself, Janet. He's looking at my Sara."

"*Me?*"

Why would a perfectly gorgeous specimen of male hunkhood single her out in a crowd of two hundred people?

"Sara, turn around and tell us whether or not the gentleman coming this way is your date," commanded Mrs. Matthews.

She turned, the thought crossing her mind that it

would only take a moment to say that she had no idea who this man was, but some primitive instinct made the hairs at the back of her neck stand on end. Like a compass needle drawn irresistibly to a magnetic force field, her gaze zeroed in on his.

The jolt was like a shock wave slamming into her body.

She stared at him, mesmerized, unable to move or speak. Resplendent in a black tux, he resembled a magnificent beast as he took a step toward her, his movements as fluid and graceful as a jungle cat stalking its prey, his silver eyes glinting dangerously in the light.

A million thoughts, questions and accusations had run through her mind for the past two weeks but, for the life of her, she couldn't summon up a single word now. All the time she'd been writing after he'd left, punishing the Jaguar, she'd secretly fantasized this moment, of seeing him again and saying the things she should have said when he'd left her so callously that morning.

But the words stored in her mind, the words that usually spilled from her brain and filled pages upon pages, dissolved under the intensity of that hypnotic gaze.

And all the time he was coming closer, moving in for the kill. She stepped back, bumping into her mother and, suddenly, her numb brain began functioning, sifting furiously through the possibilities, searching for a quick exit.

She needed to get out of here!

But there was no escape. She was surrounded on all sides by her mother's friends clamoring for an introduction.

Her panic must have been evident on her face because his mouth curved up in amusement, as though he'd read her thoughts.

Running again?

Yes, damn you! she wanted to scream. She wanted to get far away from him, from the crazy, riotous emotions he triggered inside her, and from the foolish, pea-brained idiot she became when he was within kissing distance. She wanted to dig a deep hole and dive in. She wanted to go back to her safe little cottage in Beaver Creek.

She wanted to be a coward again.

But he wouldn't let her, her mother wouldn't let her, the hormone-crazed women around her wouldn't let her and, most of all, she wouldn't let herself.

Tossing a defiant look at him, she stood her ground.

His smile widened.

She squared her shoulders and pasted on an answering smile that in reality was nothing more than muscle exercise. She then closed the distance between them, extending her arms to greet him. Dakota took her proffered hands, drawing her close. She took a deep, steadying breath and before she knew it, she was only inches away from his compelling warmth. She needed space between them, more space than this ballroom offered. In a jerky motion, she withdrew from him, kissing the air around his ears like she had seen her mother do a million times before whispering words of greeting.

"What the hell are you doing here?"

"I couldn't very well let you come unescorted, could I?"

"Cut the Sir Galahad crap. It's not going to work this time."

"You wound me, love."

"Good. Now get lost."

"Smile, sweetheart. You wouldn't want these lovely ladies to get the wrong impression, would you?"

"I mean it. Get lost or I'll sic 'em on you."

His eyes narrowed. "You wouldn't."

"Oh yeah?" She smiled evilly. "Watch me."

11

SARA WASN'T quite sure how it had happened.

She'd introduced him to her mother and her mother's friends, gleefully anticipating sneaking away and leaving him to fend for himself amid a pack of ravenous women. Only he'd unleashed his arsenal of charm and that lethal smile of his and the next thing she knew, her mother was ushering them into the library on his request. And now here she was, standing in front of her father's mahogany desk, staring at him as he moved across the width of the library, excruciatingly aware of the fact that they were very much alone. Turning away before he could glimpse the vulnerability in her eyes, she began to shuffle the papers on her father's desk. "All right, you got what you wanted."

"Not quite yet, but I will." His voice, so very close behind her, was soft and determined.

"We're alone now, so just say whatever it is you have to say and get out."

"Aren't you going to ask me why I've come back?"

She felt his breath warm against her ear, the heat of his body pressing against the back of her legs, enticing her, tempting her to just give up and lean into his strength. But she'd come too far, had paid too high a price to be taken in again.

"I don't care why you've come back," she lied, the

papers rustling in her shaking fingers. "All I'm interested in is seeing you leave."

"But I'm not interested in leaving, Sara. We still have some unfinished business between us."

She slammed the papers on the desk and whirled around to face him. "There is no business between us, finished or unfinished. You made that quite clear before you left and if I had any doubts, they disappeared when you cashed that check!"

"Ah, yes, the infamous check." His eyes kindled into silver flames. "I was wondering when we'd get around to that. You have quite a way with words, honey. 'For services rendered' has a certain, unmistakable ring to it, doesn't it?"

She lifted her chin in defiance, even as an embarrassed heat crept up her cheeks. "You cashed it, so now we're even. I don't owe you a thing, including an explanation."

A dangerous, predatory gleam appeared in his eyes. "But that's where you're wrong, Sara. I think you owe me an apology."

"An apology?" she sputtered, staring disbelievingly at the remarkably calm expression on his face. "You want *me* to apologize to *you*?"

"That's right. I told you once that what's between us has nothing to do with money, remember?"

"Is that the only reason you came back? To jog my memory?"

"Maybe I just wanted to get back at you. To make you feel as angry as I did when I opened that envelope."

"I see," she said, her voice emotionless as she stared at one of the tiny black buttons in the middle of his chest, but she knew the tears trickling down her cheeks betrayed her hurt.

She heard him release his breath in a long sigh before he tipped up her chin with his finger, forcing her to meet his steady regard. Patiently, he wiped the tears from her cheeks with his thumbs. "The truth is that I missed you, Sara. I missed talking to you and laughing with you. I missed your smile and I missed the way you make me crazy sometimes. But most of all, I missed being inside you, loving you."

She stared up at him in utter disbelief.

"Did you miss me?" he asked softly.

"No! I—"

"Liar," he murmured, caressing her cheek.

She opened her mouth to protest, and his gaze fell to her lips. His thumb followed, rubbing back and forth in sinfully slow strokes. "It feels like years since I've touched you," he whispered.

Her breath caught in her throat at the naked hunger in his eyes and ripples of treacherous heat pooled in her belly.

"And forever since I've kissed you..."

His lips touched hers in a kiss as soft and gentle as summer rain. Sara closed her eyes in helpless passion as he pressed light, feathery kisses into the sensitive curve of her throat. It had been so long since he'd held her and she needed him so much. Silently, she acknowledged to herself that she still loved him, wanted him with a depth and ferocity that humbled her.

"Love me, Dakota," she whispered.

"I do, Sara. I do," he groaned, amazed anew at the intensity of longing that swept over him whenever she was near. And then he was folding her into his arms and devouring her mouth in a hungry kiss. He skimmed a hand across the lush curve of her hip and over her stomach, sliding it upward until he cupped a ripe, chiffon-covered breast. She clutched desperately at his chest, his shoulders, his hair, a low moan escaping her lips when he brushed his knuckles across a sensitive tip. It swelled to the touch, forming a tiny nub which he longed to take into his mouth and tease with his tongue.

"Where's the zip, honey?"

She guided his hand to the side of her dress. Seconds later, the bodice of her gown fell miraculously to her waist and he lifted her breasts out of the filmy confines of her bra.

"So beautiful," he murmured, nuzzling and teasing the creamy globes with their enticing pink crests.

She arched her back, thrusting a perfect peak toward his mouth. "Please..."

"You don't know how many times I've dreamed of this, love."

Sara dug her nails into his back as his warm mouth finally closed over an aching nipple, her knees nearly giving way at the intensely erotic sensations that flooded her. Everywhere he touched, a hot flame burst to life. The fire licked at her skin, heated her blood, until she was burning with a white-hot fever.

Frantically, she pulled his mouth back to hers. "I want you, Dakota. I want you inside me...filling me...like you did before...."

He groaned at the provocative images conjured by her words, his arousal straining for release. "I want it too...so damned much I think I'm going to explode."

"Then come inside me."

Her whispered command was more temptation than he could withstand. Whenever he was around her, his self-control seemed to shatter into a million insignificant pieces. But he didn't care because this was what made being with Sara so unpredictable and infuriating, yet so exciting and arousing. She affected him as no other woman ever had, or ever would. He would never tire of her, of her smile and her laughter, of touching her and loving her.

His hand, trembling with emotion, shimmied under her gown and slid up her legs, gliding over silky, thigh-high stockings and softly rounded hips, and rimmed the edge of her panties. His fingers tangled in her damp curls and skimmed down to touch her. She was hot and wet and ready, her body shivering in his arms as she pressed herself against his hand.

"Now," she breathed. "Oh please, do it now!"

"Yes." He reached down with one hand to free himself, then fumbled in his pocket for protection. By the time he managed to get it on, his breathing had become harsh and labored, and his hands were shaking with the force of his need.

"Hurry!"

He discarded the little scrap of silk that was the only barrier between them now and then his hands were at her waist, lifting her up and lowering her onto him. She was hot and tight and slick, welcoming him with a sigh, wrapping her satiny legs around his waist. He cupped her buttocks and held her firmly to him.

"Give me your mouth, baby, and hold tight," he whispered as he walked toward the door.

Each step he took was exquisite torture for Sara, each new jolt a sweet agony, and by the time he'd reached the door and turned the lock, she was straining, gasping, on the edge of exploding. Then, suddenly, her back was to the door and he was thrusting, quick, hard strokes that had her crying out her pleasure.

She arched, his hair clenched in her fists as the pressure built to a fever pitch. He drove harder, faster, once, twice, three times, and then she was crashing, screaming, coming, as wave upon wave of pure, wild rapture swept over and drowned her in pleasure.

He felt her climax, felt her body ripple and contract around him in shuddering waves, heard her passionate cries of release against his shoulder, and it was like touching a flame to a trail of gasoline. The fire rushed through him like a bullet through the barrel of a gun and he exploded inside her with a hoarse cry.

"HONEY, I think you just killed me," he murmured against her hair when he had the strength, his chest still heaving with exertion.

She buried her face in his throat, her breath warm against his skin. "It's no more than you deserve."

"Ah, but what a way to go."

She began to laugh, a bold, sexy laugh that made him yearn to love her again. "I can't believe we just did that."

He smiled, pressing a tender kiss on her cheek. "What? Made love against the door of your parents' library with two hundred people milling around on the other side? What's not to believe?"

As soon as the words *made love* came out of his mouth, he knew he'd made a mistake. She lifted her head, her dark eyes staring into his, and her laughter faded.

"Was that what it was?" she whispered. "Making love?"

The haunted look on her face sent a shaft of pain ripping through him, and he closed his eyes and held her tightly, thankful that he'd come to his senses in the nick of time, thankful that she was in his arms now, thankful that there was still a chance to make this right.

"Dakota?"

He opened his eyes to find her looking up at him with concern.

Sighing, he leaned his forehead against hers. "I've been a jackass, haven't I?"

She nodded wordlessly.

"Loch thinks I'm lovesick."

"And what do you think?" she asked softly.

"I think that, for once in his misbegotten life, he may be right."

"I see."

"And I'm not allowed to come home until I find a cure. Luckily," he said, reaching into the inside pocket of his jacket and pulling out a small velvet box, "I have a plan."

"A plan," she repeated, staring speechlessly at the box.

"Open it."

With trembling fingers, Sara lifted the lid, uncovering a stunning star-shaped diamond ring nestled against the dark blue velvet.

"Well?" he asked.

She looked blankly up at him. "Well what?"

His gray eyes gleamed with laughter. "Sara Matthews, will you marry me?"

"You really want to marry me?"

The laughter faded, replaced by an unbelievably tender expression as he caressed her cheek. "Oh, yes."

"Because we have explosive sex together?"

"Because I love you."

"Oh."

"And because you're sexy and intelligent and inquisitive and irritating and adorable and because your smile turns me on. I need you, Sara, more than I've ever needed anyone or anything, and I want to spend the rest of my life making love to you and answering your unending supply of questions."

"Oh."

"Is that all you have to say?"

"No."

"Is that a no, you won't marry me, or no, that's not all you have to say?"

"It's a no, that's not all I have to say."

"I was afraid of that."

"You put me through the worst two weeks of my life, you big lummox," she said as he slid the ring onto her finger, "and I'm going to take perverse pleasure in making sure you pay for it for the rest of our lives."

"Let me hear you say the words, Sara," he whispered, as she wrapped her arms around his neck.

"Yes, you may spend the rest of your life making love to me and answering my unending supply of questions. And you can start right now. What did you do with the money from the check?"

"Those weren't the words I was hoping to hear," he said dryly.

"Quit stalling, Wilder."

"I used it to buy something for you."

"My ring?"

He rolled his eyes. "Give me some credit."

"What then?"

He dangled a set of keys in front of her. "Let's just say it's guaranteed to give you the best ride on two wheels."

Realization dawned and she stared incredulously at him for a moment. "You bought me a motorcycle?"

"Not just any motorcycle. A Harley. And technically, you bought it for yourself. As soon as we get home to the Macota, you're going to learn how to ride it."

Laughing, Sara reached up, pulled his face down and kissed him with all the love and longing and happiness in her heart.

The manhunt was officially over.

Head Down Under for twelve tales of heated romance in beautiful and untamed Australia!

Here's a sneak preview of the first novel in THE AUSTRALIANS

Outback Heat by Emma Darcy
available July 1998

'HAVE I DONE something wrong?' Angie persisted, wishing Taylor would emit a sense of camaraderie instead of holding an impenetrable reserve.

'Not at all,' he assured her. 'I would say a lot of things right. You seem to be fitting into our little Outback community very well. I've heard only good things about you.'

'They're nice people,' she said sincerely. Only the Maguire family kept her shut out of their hearts.

'Yes,' he agreed. 'Though I appreciate it's taken considerable effort from you. It is a world away from what you're used to.'

The control Angie had been exerting over her feelings snapped. He wasn't as blatant as his aunt in his prejudice against her but she'd felt it coming through every word he'd spoken and she didn't deserve any of it.

'Don't judge me by your wife!'

His jaw jerked. A flicker of some dark emotion destroyed the steady power of his probing gaze.

'No two people are the same. If you don't know that, you're a man of very limited vision. So I come from the city as your wife did! That doesn't stop me from being an individual in my own right.'

She straightened up, proudly defiant, furiously angry with the situation. 'I'm *me*. Angie Cordell. And it's time you took the blinkers off your eyes, Taylor Maguire.'

Then she whirled away from him, too agitated by the explosive expulsion of her emotion to keep facing him.

The storm outside hadn't yet eased. There was nowhere to go. She stopped at the window, staring blindly at the torrential rain. The thundering on the roof was almost deafening but it wasn't as loud as the silence behind her.

'You want me to go, don't you? You've given me a month's respite and now you want me to leave and channel my energies somewhere else.'

'I didn't say that, Angie.'

'You were working your way around it.' Bitterness at his tactics spewed the suspicion. 'Do you have your first choice of governess waiting in the wings?'

'No. I said I'd give you a chance.'

'Have you?' She swung around to face him. 'Have you really, Taylor?'

He hadn't moved. He didn't move now except to make a gesture of appeasement. 'Angie, I was merely trying to ascertain how you felt.'

'Then let me tell you your cynicism was shining through every word.'

He frowned, shook his head. 'I didn't mean to hurt you.' The blue eyes fastened on hers with devastating sincerity. 'I truly did not come in here to take you down or suggest you leave.'

Her heart jiggled painfully. He might be speaking the truth but the judgements were still there, the judgements that ruled his attitude towards her, that kept her shut out of his life, denied any real sharing with him, denied his confidence and trust. She didn't know why it meant so much to her but it did. It did. And the need to fight for justice from him was as much a raging torrent inside her as the rain outside.

MEN at WORK

All work and no play? Not these men!

April 1998

KNIGHT SPARKS by Mary Lynn Baxter

Sexy lawman Rance Knight made a career of arresting the bad guys. Somehow, though, he thought policewoman Carly Mitchum was framed. Once they'd uncovered the truth, could Rance let Carly go...or would he make a citizen's arrest?

May 1998

HOODWINKED by Diana Palmer

CEO Jake Edwards donned coveralls and went undercover as a mechanic to find the saboteur in his company. Nothing—or no one—would distract him, not even beautiful secretary Maureen Harris. Jake had to catch the thief—*and* the woman who'd stolen his heart!

June 1998

DEFYING GRAVITY by Rachel Lee

Tim O'Shaughnessy and his business partner, Liz Pennington, had always been close—but never *this* close. As the danger of their assignment escalated, so did their passion. When the job was over, could they ever go back to business as usual?

MEN AT WORK™

Available at your favorite retail outlet!

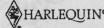 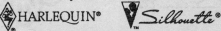

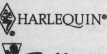

DEBBIE MACOMBER

invites you to the

HEART OF TEXAS

Join Debbie Macomber as she brings you the lives
and loves of the folks in the ranching community
of Promise, Texas.

If you loved Midnight Sons—don't miss
Heart of Texas! A brand-new six-book series
from Debbie Macomber.

Available in February 1998
at your favorite retail store.

Heart of Texas by Debbie Macomber

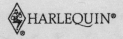

HARLEQUIN®

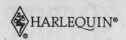

Not The Same Old Story!

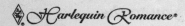

Exciting, glamorous
romance stories that take
readers around the world.

Sparkling, fresh and ten-
der love stories that
bring you pure romance.

Bold and adventurous—
Temptation is strong women,
bad boys, great sex!

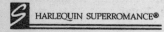

Provocative and realistic
stories that celebrate life
and love.

Contemporary
fairy tales—where
anything is possible
and where dreams
come true.

Heart-stopping, suspenseful
adventures that combine the
best of romance and mystery.

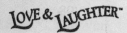

Humorous and romantic stories
that capture the lighter side of
love.

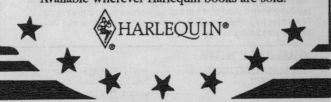

Presents Extravaganza

25 YEARS!

It's our birthday and we're celebrating....

Twenty-five years of romance fiction
featuring men of the world and captivating women—
Seduction and passion guaranteed!

Not only are we promising you three months of terrific
books, authors and romance, but as an added **bonus**
with the retail purchase of two Presents® titles,
you can receive a special one-of-a-kind keepsake.
It's our gift to you!

Look in the back pages of any Harlequin Presents® title,
from May to July 1998, for more details.

Available wherever Harlequin books are sold.

HARLEQUIN®

HARLEQUIN®

Temptation®

COMING NEXT MONTH